雅典文化

小小一本，讓你輕・鬆・說英語！

1000 基礎實用單字

張瑜凌◎編著

只要掌握基礎單字，輕鬆開口說英語！

NEW BASIC VO... 10...

若是想要順利掌控英語的口語，你就必須具備基礎字彙使用能力
語言的形成必須仰賴字彙為基礎

本書編撰了生活中使用最頻繁的單字
以不同詞性分類單字讓你輕鬆掌握
真人發音讓你輕鬆學習正確發音

MP3

前言

只要掌握基礎單字，輕鬆開口說英語！

語言的形成必須仰賴字彙為基礎。因此，若是想要能夠順利掌控英語的口語使用，就必須具備基礎字彙的使用能力。

但是這麼多的單字，該具備哪一些單字呢？很簡單，只要以「生活常用會話」為使用依歸，如此一來，那些在英語中使用最頻繁的單字，便是您首要必須要具備的單字。

「1000 基礎實用單字」編撰了生活中使用最頻繁的基礎單字，分別以不同詞性及單字附錄羅列在本書中，您可以依照詞性的不同，進而分門別類的背誦。

建議您依照本書所附的 MP3 學習光碟，先學習基礎單字的正確發音，然後逐句學習會話的應用方式。跟隨外籍教師口語會話的頻率伴讀，口語會話的能力及技巧將更為流暢，以達到日益進步的學習成果。

關於本書

這是一本能夠讓您在學習單字的同時，還能同時學習口語會話的語言工具書。

除了單字本身的音標、中文解釋之外，本書還額外編撰「同義」、「反義」、「類似」的單字提示，以方便您學習時，能同時記憶相關單字。

每一個單字均有「例句」及「會話」兩段內容，可供您學習應用。

詞性

縮寫	中文詞性	原文
n.	名詞	noun
pron.	代名詞	pronoun
adj.	形容詞	adjective
v.	動詞	verb
aux.	助動詞	auxiliary
adv.	副詞	adverb
prep.	介係詞	preposition
conj.	連接詞	conjunction
p.	過去式	past
pp.	過去分詞	pastparticiple
ppr.	現在分詞	presentparticiple

本書還有「深入分析」單元，針對單字的使用與相關注意事項，有更深入的解析與應用說明，提供您在學習的過程中，能夠更有效率地應用在口語會話中。

目錄

名詞篇 Chapter 1

目錄

形容詞篇

Chapter 2

目錄

目錄

動詞篇 Chapter 3

目錄

目錄

目錄

副詞篇 Chapter 4

NEW BASIC
VOCABULARY
1000

CHAPTER 01

名詞篇

TRACK 1

it

[ɪt]

pron.　指已提及的人、事、物；（表時間、氣候、距離等無人稱動詞的主詞）這、那、它

相關　its pron. 它的

例句

It's not difficult to learn English.
學英文不是難事。

It's very hot today.
今天很熱。

會話

A : What's this?
這是什麼？

B : It's a map of Taiwan.
這是台灣地圖。

A : It's the most horrible thing I've ever seen.
這是我見過最恐怖的事了。

B : I know. It's not easy for you.
我知道。難為你了。

this

[ðɪs]
adj. pron.　這個（人、事、物）
(pl. these)

反義 that adj. pron. **那個**

例句

Who told you this?
這事是誰告訴你的？

You look in this box here.
你查看這裡的這個盒子。

會話

A : Is this a present?
這是個禮物嗎？

B : Yes, it's for my wife.
是的，要給我太太的。

A : Why are you doing this?
你為什麼要這麼做？

B : It's none of your business.
不關你的事。

that

[ðæt]
pron. adj. 那、那個（人、事、物）
(pl. those)

反義 this pron. adj. 這個

例句

Who told you that story?
誰告訴你那個故事的？

Look at that.
瞧瞧那個！

會話

A : That's impossible.
不可能的！

B : You really think so?
你真的這麼認為？

A : That is my mother.
那是我媽媽。

B : She looks so young.
她看起來好年輕。

today

[tə'de]
n. 今天、現在、當代
adv. 在今天、在當代

反義 yesterday n. adv. **昨天**

例句

Today is my birthday!
今天是我的生日！

Are you going shopping today?
你（們）今天要去逛街購物嗎？

會話

A : What are you going to do today?
你們今天要做什麼？

B : We're going to swim.
我們要去游泳。

A : This is a good idea.
這個主意不錯。

B : You mean we can go to a movie today?
你是說我們今天可以去看電影囉？

tomorrow

[tə'mɔro]
n. 明天、未來
adv. （在）明天

例句

We are going to a party tomorrow.
明天我們要去參加一個派對。

Tomorrow is Sunday.
明天是星期天。

會話

A : How about tomorrow?
明天如何？

B : Sure. What time?
好啊！幾點鐘？

A : The day after tomorrow is my birthday.
後天是我的生日。

B : What present do you want?
你想要什麼禮物？

yesterday

[ˈjɛstɚde]
n. 昨天、最近、近來
adv. （在）昨天、近來

例句

We had no classes yesterday.
昨天我們沒課。

He went out the day before yesterday.
他前天出去的。

會話

A : When did you see David?
你什麼時候遇見大衛的？

B : I saw him at yesterday's meeting.
我是在昨天的會議上見到他的。

A : Yesterday was my birthday.
昨天是我的生日。

B : Really? You didn't tell me.
真的？你沒有告訴我。

tonight

[tə'naɪt]
n. 今夜、今晚
adv. 在今晚

例句

What's on TV tonight?
今晚有什麼電視節目？

Tonight will be rainy.
今晚會下雨。

會話

A : What are you going to do tonight?
你們今天晚上要做什麼？

B : We're going to a concert.
我們要去聽音樂會。

A : It's chilly tonight, isn't it?
今晚冷斃了，對嗎？

B : Yeah, but I like it.
是啊，但是我喜歡。

morning

['mɔrnɪŋ]
n. 早上、早晨、上午

例句

We usually go shopping on friday mornings.
我們總是在星期五上午逛街購物。

What did you do in the morning?
早上你做了什麼事？

會話

A : Did David call you this morning?
大衛今天早上有打電話給你嗎？

B : No. Why?
沒有。為什麼（這麼問）？

A : I'm going to do my homework in the morning.
我要在早上做我的功課。

B : Don't you think it's too late?
你不覺得太晚了嗎？

afternoon

['æftə'nun]
n. 下午、午後

例句

We have no classes this afternoon.
我們今天下午不用上課。

David often comes in the afternoon.
大衛下午常來。

會話

A : It's a warm and beautiful Sunday afternoon.
今天是個風和日麗的星期天午後。

B : Yes, it is.
是啊，沒錯！

A : How about this afternoon? I'll pick you up.
今天下午好嗎？我會來接你。

B : This afternoon would be fine.
今天下午可以。

evening

['ivnɪŋ]

n. 傍晚、晚間

相 關 night n. 夜晚

例句

I'll do my homework in the evening.
我將在晚上做我的作業。

Good evening.
晚安。(晚上與人道別時用 Good night)

會話

A : When wiil you do your homework?
你要什麼時候做你的功課?

B : I'll do my homework in the evening.
我會在晚上做我的功課。

A : You'd better not go out in the evening.
你最好不要在晚上出門。

B : Why not?
為什麼不要?

child

[tʃaɪld]
n. 孩子、兒童
（pl. children ['tʃɪldrən]）

類 似 kid n. 孩童

例句

April the fourth is Children's Day.
四月四日是兒童節。

Three children are playing on the playground.
三個小孩正在操場上玩耍。

會話

A : How many children do you have?
你有幾個小孩？

B : I have two sons.
我有兩個兒子。

A : You don't have children, do you?
你沒有小孩，對嗎？

B : No, I don't.
沒有，我沒有。

color

[ˈkʌlɚ]
n. 顏色

例句

What color do you have?
你們有什麼顏色？

It comes in many colors.
這個有許多種顏色。

會話

A : What color is your car?
你的車子是什麼顏色？

B : It's black.
是黑色。

A : What color do you want to paint?
你想要漆成什麼顏色？

B : How about black?
你覺得黑色怎麼樣？

food

[fud]

n. 食物、食品、(精神的)糧食

例句

Many sweet foods are on sale in the store.
這家商店的許多種甜食在特價中。

Books are food for the mind.
書是心靈的食糧。

會話

A : Is there any food to eat? I'm so hungry.
有吃的嗎?我好餓!

B : Let me make you a sandwich.
我幫你做一個三明治。

A : How much junk food have you eaten today?
你今天吃了多少垃圾食物?

B : Nope. I hate junk food.
沒有啊!我討厭垃圾食物。

dinner

['dɪnɚ]
n. 正餐、晚餐

類 似 supper n. 晚飯

例句

We are having fish for dinner.
我們晚飯會吃魚。

I like to watch TV after dinner.
我喜歡在晚飯後看電視。

會話

A : Would you like to have dinner with me?
要和我一起吃晚餐嗎？

B : Sure, why not?
好啊，為什麼不？

A : You can come over and cook dinner for me.
你可以過來幫我煮晚餐。

B : Why me?
為什麼是我？

foot

[fʊt]
n. 腳、足、英尺（pl. feet〔fit〕）

例句

I often go to school on foot.
我經常走路去上學。

A small house stood at the foot of the mountain.
山腳下有棟小房子。

會話

A : How tall is the guy?
那傢伙有多高？

B : He's very tall. Maybe seven feet.
他很高，可能有 7 英尺。

A : Is it far from here?
離這裡遠嗎？

B : No, not at all. You can get there on foot.
不，一點都不會。你可以走路過去。

home

[hom]
n. 家
adv. 在家地、回家地

例句

On my way home I saw David.
在我回家的路上，我看到了大衛。

Make yourself at home.
請不要拘束。

會話

A : It's pretty late now.
現在很晚了。

B : Yes, it is. Let's go home.
是啊，的確是！我們回家吧！

A : Is David around?
大衛在嗎？

B : He's not at home now.
他現在不在家。

name

[nem]
n. 名字、姓名、名稱
v. 命名

例句

What's the name of that river?
那條河叫什麼名字？

They named the baby Elizabeth.
他們為嬰孩取名伊莉莎白。

會話

A : May I have your name, please?
請問你的大名？

B : I'm David White.
我是大衛・懷特。

A : What's her name?
她叫什麼名字？

B : Her name is Mary.
她的名字是瑪麗。

nobody

['nobadɪ]

n. 沒有人、誰也不、無足輕重者

pron. 沒有人、誰也不

例句

There's nobody here.
這裡一個人也沒有。

Nobody could speak Japanese.
沒有人會說日語。

會話

A : Help!
救命啊！

B : Come on. Nobody would hear you.
得了吧！沒有人會聽見的。

A : Why don't you like him?
為什麼你不喜歡他？

B : Him? He's a nobody.
他？他只是個泛泛之輩。

nothing

['nʌθɪŋ]
pron. n. 沒有東西、沒有什麼

例句

There is nothing good in the evening newspaper.
晚報上沒什麼好消息。

We could see nothing but fog.
除了霧，我們什麼都看不見。

會話

A : Something wrong?
有問題嗎？

B : Nothing.
沒事！

A : What did you see?
你看見什麼？

B : Nothing but trees.
除了樹，什麼都沒看見。

anything

['ɛnɪˌθɪŋ]

pron. 任何事物、一些事物

例句

Is there anything in that room?
那房間裡有什麼東西？

Anything else?
還有什麼別的事嗎？

會話

A : Do you have anything to say?
你有什麼話要說的嗎？

B : Nothing at all.
完全沒有！

A : Anything wrong?
有問題嗎？

B : Yeah, there's a thief in our house.
是啊，我們的房子裡有一個小偷。

everyone

['ɛvrɪ,wʌn]
pron. 每人、人人

例句

Does anyone like it?
有人喜歡它嗎？

Everyone wants to attend the concert.
每個人都想參加音樂會。

會話

A : How is your family?
你家人好嗎？

B : Everyone is fine.
大家都很好！

A : I dislike Maria.
我不喜歡瑪莉亞。

B : Why? Because everyone likes her?
為什麼？因為每個人都喜歡她？

everything

['ɛvrɪ,θɪŋ]

pron. 每件事、每樣東西

例句

Everything is ready now for the party.
派對的一切都已準備就緒。

We have done everything possible to help her.
我們已盡了全力來幫助她。

會話

A : I really worry about this plan.
我真的很擔心這個計畫。

B : Come on, everything will be fine.
不要這樣，沒問題的。

A : How is everything?
事情都還好嗎？

B : Everything's fine.
凡事都很好。

someone

['sʌm,wʌn]

pron. 有人、某人

例句

You'd better ask someone to help you.
你最好請個人來幫你。

Are you expecting someone this afternoon?
今天下午你是不是在等什麼人？

會話

A : Did I have any message?
有我的留言嗎？

B : Yes. Someone left this for you.
有的。有人把這個留給你。

A : Someone told me you were gone.
有人告訴我你失蹤了。

B : But here I am.
但是我在這裡啊！

something

['sʌmθɪŋ]

pron. 某事（物）

例句

I was looking for something cheaper.
我正在找較便宜的東西。

Something wrong?
有問題嗎？

會話

A : Are you looking for something?
你在找什麼嗎？

B : Yes, I'd like to buy a tie.
是的，我要買領帶。

A : Something different from this?
和這個有不同嗎？

B : This one is much bigger.
這一個大多了！

thing

[θɪŋ]

n. 事、物、事情、情況

例句

No one can do two things at once.
一心不可二用。

Put your things away.
把你的東西收拾整齊。

會話

A : Things will get better soon.
情況很快就會好轉。

B : Thank you for being with me.
謝謝你陪著我。

A : Things became complicated.
事情變得複雜了！

B : Why? What makes you think so?
為什麼？你為什麼會這麼想？

time

[taɪm]

n. 時間、鐘點、一段時間、次、次數

例句

What time is it now?
現在幾點鐘了？

It took us a long time to go there on foot.
我們走了很長的一段時間才到那裡。

會話

A : Can you type this letter for me?
你可以幫我將這封信打字嗎？

B : I don't have so much time.
我沒那麼多時間。

A : Now listen, I have to...
現在聽好，我必須要…

B : It's OK. I understand you don't have time for me.
沒關係！我瞭解你沒時間陪我。

last

[læst]
n. 最後、死期、最近的東西
v. 持續、耐久、足夠
adj. 最後的、剛過去的、最近一次的
adv. 最後地、最近地

例句

David was the last to arrive.
大衛是最後一個到達的人。

When did you last see him?
你上一次見到他是什麼時候？

會話

A : How long will it last?
會維持多久？

B : About 2 weeks.
大約兩個星期。

A : Wow, it takes so much time.
哇，要花好多時間。

B : Yeah, I know.
是啊，我知道。

middle

['mɪdl̩]

n. 中部、中間、中途

例句

He planted rose trees in the middle of the garden.
他把玫瑰花種在花園的中間。

I'm in the middle school.
我正在讀中學。

會話

A : Are you busy now?
你現在在忙嗎？

B : I'm in the middle of something.
我正在忙。

A : Hi, honey, just wondering what you are doing.
嗨，親愛的，我在想你正在做什麼？

B : I'm in the middle of a tennis game.
我正在忙著玩網球遊戲。

moment

['momənt]
n. 一會兒、片刻、瞬間

同 義 second n. 片刻

例句

It'll only take a moment.
這件事只需要片刻的時間。
Both of them arrived at the same moment.
他們倆同時到達。

會話

A : Can I talk to John?
我能和約翰說話嗎？
B : He's busy at the moment.
他現在正在忙。

A : Wait a moment, please.
請稍候。
B : No problem.
沒問題。

problem

['prabləm]

n. 問題、難題

類 似 question n. 問題

例句

The workers are discussing a problem.
工人們正在討論一個難題。

He'll solve the problem.
他將會解決這個問題。

會話

A : Any problems?
有問題嗎？

B : Nope. Everything is fine.
沒事！一切都沒問題。

A : What's your problem?
你的問題是什麼？

B : It's about my summer vacation.
是有關我的暑假。

question

['kwɛstʃən]

n. 問題、質問、論點、疑點

v. 詢問、審問、對…表示疑問

反義 answer n. v. 回答

例句

Do you have any questions?
你（們）有什麼問題嗎？

The question is why?
問題是為什麼？

會話

A : No more questions?
沒有任何問題了嗎？

B : I have one more question.
我還有一個問題。

A : What's your question?
你的問題是什麼？

B : It's about my salary.
是有關我的薪水。

trouble

['trʌbl̩]

n. 困難、煩惱、麻煩

例句

I'm sorry for the trouble I'm giving you.
給你添麻煩實在抱歉。

You're really a trouble maker.
你真是麻煩製造者。

會話

A : I'm in trouble. Can you help me?
我有麻煩了，你能幫我嗎？

B : Sure, what is it?
好啊，什麼事？

A : You're asking for trouble.
你是在自找麻煩。

B : Sorry for that.
（我為那件事感到）抱歉啦！

right

[raɪt]
n. 右、右邊
adj. 右邊的、正確的
adv. 向右地、正確地、完全地

反 義 left n. adj. adv. 左、左面、向左

例句

Is that the right time?
那是正確的時間嗎？

Turn right at the crossing.
在十字路口向右轉。

會話

A : How should I do it?
我應該怎麼做？

B : Go right back to the beginning.
直接回到開始處。

A : It's on your right side.
在你的右手邊。

B : I see. Thank you.
我瞭解。謝謝你。

decision

[dɪ'sɪʒən]
n. 決定、決心、果斷

例句

You'll have to make a decision whether to go with us or not.
你得決定是否和我們一起去。

He lacks decision and finally missed the chance.
他缺乏果斷，最終錯過了這次機會。

會話

A : I think you have made the wrong decision.
我認為你做了一個錯誤的決定。

B : You really think so?
你真這麼認為？

A : I don't know what to do.
我不知道該怎麼辦。

B : Come on. You're the decision maker.
得了吧！你是做決定的人。

exercise

['ɛksɚ,saɪz]

n. 鍛鍊、運動、練習、習題（可數名詞）

例句

If you don't get more exercise you'll get fat.
如果你不多做運動，你就會變胖。

I'm doing exercises in English grammar.
我正在做英語文法的練習。

會話

A : What did the doctor say?
醫生說什麼？

B : He told me to do more exercise.
他告訴我要多做運動。

A : How often do you do exercise?
你有多常做運動？

B : I go swimming every week.
我每週去游泳。

experience

[ɪk'spɪrɪəns]

n. 經驗、體驗、經歷

例句

Experience is our best teacher.
經驗是我們最好的老師。

He gained experience in teaching.
他得到教學經驗。

會話

A : I have much experience in teaching English.
我對英語教學有豐富的經驗。
B : Well, can you teach me English?
那麼你可以教我英文嗎？

A : Did you have any experiences on your trip?
你的旅途中有任何特別的經歷嗎？
B : Yes, I had a lot of interesting experiences.
有啊，我有很多有趣的經歷。

fact

[fækt]

n. 事實、實際、真相

同 義 truth n. 事實、實情、實話

例句

In fact, I'm sure that's the only satisfactory way out.
事實上，我認為那是唯一令人滿意的出路。

As a matter of fact, I don't know what you're talking about.
事實上，我不知道你在說什麼。

會話

A : Tell me the truth.
告訴我實情。

B : The fact is that he's lost his job.
事實是他丟了工作。

A : Is it the fact that he is our general manager?
他是我們的總經理，這是真的嗎？

B : Yes, that's right.
是的，沒錯。

favor

['fevɚ]

n. 恩惠、好意、幫助、贊同

同 義 help n. v. 幫助

例句

Will you do me a favor by turning the radio down?

能幫個忙把收音機關小聲一點嗎？

I want to ask a favor of you: will you lend me your car?

請你幫個忙 ： 把你的汽車借給我好嗎？

會話

A : Would you please do me a favor?

你願意幫我忙嗎？

B : Sure. What is it?

好啊！什麼事？

A : Are you in favor of gun control?

你贊成實行槍支管制嗎？

B : Yes, I am.

是的，我贊成。

advice

[əd'vaɪs]
n. 忠告、意見、消息

同 義 suggestion n. 建議

例句

He gave me his advice.
他給了我一些他的忠告。
The doctor gave him advice to have a complete rest.
醫生勸他要多多休息。

會話

A : Do you want my advice?
你要我的建議嗎？
B : Thanks. I don't need it.
多謝了！我不需要。

A : What did you say to him?
你對他說什麼？
B : I gave him advice to give up smoking.
我勸他要戒菸。

idea

[aɪ'diə]

n. 瞭解、想法、思想、觀念、概念

同 義 thought n. **想法、見解**

例句

I've got a good idea of what he wants.
他想要什麼我很清楚。

He'll have his own ideas about that.
那件事他會有自己的想法。

會話

A : Maybe we should pick her up at her place.
也許我們應該去她家接她。

B : What a good idea! Let's go.
好主意！走吧。

A : Do you have any idea of what I'm trying to explain?
你瞭解我所要解釋的意思嗎？

B : No. What's the point?
不瞭解。重點是什麼？

bath

[bæθ]
n. 洗澡、沐浴、浴室、浴缸

例句

Why don't you take a bath?
你何不洗個澡？

When I got home, I had a hot bath and went to bed immediately.
我回到家後，洗個熱水澡，然後就馬上上床睡覺了。

會話

A : I often take a cold bath in the morning.
我經常在早上洗冷水澡。

B : Isn't it cold?
不會冷嗎？

A : You are home early.
你今天早提回來。

B : I'm tired. I wanna have a bath.
我很累。我想洗個澡。

chance

[tʃæns]
n. 機會、可能性、偶然性

同義 opportunity n. 機會

例句

There is little chance of meeting him again.
要和他再見面是不太可能的事了。

Chance plays an important part in many card games.
在許多紙牌遊戲中，運氣扮演著重要的角色。

會話

A : Don't you think it's a good chance?
你不覺得這是個好機會嗎？

B : Not to me.
對我來說不是。

A : There's a chance that I'll see him.
我有一個可以和他見面的好機會。

B : Good for you. Just ask him to believe you.
對你來說是好事。只要要求他相信你。

kind

[kaɪnd]
n. 種、類
adj. 友好的、和善的

例句

Haven't you got any other kinds?
你們沒有別種類型的嗎？
It's very kind of you to see me.
謝謝你來看我。

會話

A : What's this?
這是什麼？
B : This is a kind of rose.
這是一種玫瑰花。

A : Let me help you with this.
我來幫你。
B : It's very kind of you.
你真好！

who

[hu]
pron. 誰、什麼人、…的人

例句

Who won the race?
賽跑誰贏了？

The girl who spoke is my best friend.
講話的那個女孩是我最要好的朋友。

會話

A : Who is your partner?
你的伙伴是誰？

B : It's Jenny.
是珍妮。

A : Who wrote this letter to you?
誰寫這封信給你？

B : It's David.
是大衛。

NEW BASIC
VOCABULARY
1000

CHAPTER 02

形容詞篇

TRACK 2

sure

[ʃʊr]
adj. 肯定的、確信的

例句

I think so, but I'm not sure.
我是這樣想的，但是我沒有把握。

He's sure of himself.
他很有自信。

會話

A : Where is David?
大衛呢？

B : I don't know for sure.
我不太清楚。

A : Make sure you closed the door.
確定你關門了。

B : Yes, I did.
有的，我有（關）。

all

[ɔl]
adj. 整個的、全部的
adv. 全部地、完全地

例句

I'm all wet.
我全身濕透了。

They were all excited.
他們非常的激動。

會話

A : What's your plan?
你的計畫是什麼？

B : I'll do this job all my life.
我會一輩子從事這個工作。

A : Did you have fun?
你們玩得開心嗎？

B : Yes. We were all happy.
是的！我們都很高興。

any

['ɛnɪ]

adj. 一些、什麼、任何的

例句

Do you have any apples?
你（們）有蘋果嗎？

If you have any ideas about it, please tell me.
如果你有任何關於它的想法，請告訴我。

會話

A : Do you have any hats?
你們有賣帽子嗎？

B : Sure. We have some new arrivals.
當然有。我們有一些新貨剛到。

A : Do you have any children?
你有小孩嗎？

B : Yes, I have two sons.
有啊，我有兩個兒子。

beautiful

['bjutəfəl]
adj. 美麗的、漂亮的

同 義 fine adj. 美好的

例句

Mary has a beautiful skirt.
瑪麗有一條漂亮的裙子。

She's so beautiful.
她真是漂亮。

會話

A : It's a beautiful picture, isn't it?
真是一張漂亮的照片，是吧？

B : Yeah, it is.
是啊，是的。

A : Do you have children?
你有小孩嗎？

B : I have one beautiful angel.
我有一個漂亮的寶貝。

big

[bɪg]
adj. 大的、長大的

反 義 small adj. 小的

例句
We visited many big cities in Japan last week.
我們上星期訪問了日本的許多大城市。

會話
A : Do you have any big apples?
你們有（賣）大的蘋果嗎？
B : No. We only have small ones.
沒有。我們只有小的（蘋果）。

A : Wow, this birthday cake is so big.
哇，這生日蛋糕好大呀！
B : Yeah. But I like this one.
是啊！但是我喜歡這一個！

easy

['izɪ]
adj. 容易的、簡單的

反 義 hard adj. 困難的

例句

Lesson One is easier than Lesson Two.
第一課比第二課容易。

This one is easier.
這一個比較簡單。

會話

A : It's not easy for you.
難為你了。

B : Thank you for everything.
凡事多謝了！

A : It's an easy job.
這是一項簡單的工作。

B : You really think so?
你真這樣認為？

hard

[hard]
adj. 硬的、困難的、艱難的
adv. 努力地、猛烈地

同 義 difficult adj. 困難的

例句

The stone was hard.
這岩石很堅硬。

It's raining harder than ever.
現在下的雨比任何時候都大。

會話

A : What do you think?
你覺得呢？

B : This question is too hard.
這個問題太難了。

A : She's working hard.
她正在努力工作。

B : She really likes her job.
她真的很喜歡她的工作。

difficult

['dɪfə,kəlt]
adj. 困難的、不簡單的

反 義 easy adj. 容易的

例句

It is difficult to master a foreign language in a month.
要一個月之內掌握一門外語是困難的。

He is a difficult person to get along with.
他是個不好相處的人。

會話

A : It's difficult for me to do so.
要我那樣做是困難的。

B : Come on, you can make it.
不要這樣，你可以辦得到的。

A : How difficult it is.
真是難！

B : I know. It's not easy for you.
我知道。難為你了！

busy

['bɪzɪ]
adj. 忙碌的

反 義 free adj. 有空閒的

例句

What are you busy with?
你在忙什麼？

He's always busy with his work.
他總是忙於工作。

會話

A : Are you busy now?
你現在忙嗎？

B : No, not at all. What's up?
不，一點都不會。什麼事？

A : Because I'm busy now.
因為我現在正在忙。

B : Busy with what?
在忙什麼？

free

[fri]

adj. 自由的、空閒的、免費的

例句

We felt free when we moved out.
我們搬家後感到無拘無束。

He has little free time.
他很少有空閒的時間。

會話

A : Are the drinks free?
這些飲料是不是免費的？

B : No, you have to pay for them.
不是，這些飲料必須付錢。

A : Are you free now?
現在有空嗎？

B : Yes. What's up?
有啊！什麼事？

front

[frʌnt]
adj. 前面的
n. 前面、正面

反 義 back adj. 背面的

例句

There is a garden in the front of the house.
房子前面有個花園。

Write your name on the front cover.
請把你的名字寫在練習本的封面上。

會話

A : Where is the post office?
郵局在哪裡？

B : It's in front of the park.
在公園前面。

A : Where is his name?
他的名字在哪裡？

B : It's on the front cover. See?
在封面上。有看見嗎？

full

[fʊl]
adj. 充滿的、滿的、吃飽的

反 義 empty adj. 空的

例句

They had a full meal.
他們飽餐了一頓。

He got a full mark.
他得了滿分。

會話

A : Is Mr. White busy?
懷特先生在忙嗎？

B : I'm afraid so. He's got a full schedule today.
恐怕是喔！他今天的行程滿檔。

A : Do you want some cakes?
你要吃一些餅乾嗎？

B : No, thanks. I can't eat any more; I'm full up.
不，謝了。我不能再吃了，我已經飽了。

hungry

['hʌŋgrɪ]
adj. 饑餓的、渴望的

反 義 full adj. 吃飽的

例句

I'm hungry.
我餓了！

I feel a little hungry.
我覺得有點餓。

會話

A : Can I have something to eat?
有什麼可以吃的嗎？

B : Are you still hungry?
你還會餓？

A : I'm so hungry.
我好餓。

B : Let's get something to eat.
我們找點東西來吃吧！

cheap

[tʃip]
adj. 便宜的、廉價品的、不費力的

反 義 expensive adj. **昂貴的**

例句

The bag is very cheap.
這個袋子很便宜。

Talk is cheap.
說空話是不費力的。

會話

A : It's too expensive. Do you have anything cheaper?
太貴了。你有便宜一點的東西嗎？

B : That's all we have.
我們只有這些。

A : It's really cheap.
真便宜。

B : It's a real bargain.
真的很划算。

dark

[dark]
adj. 黑暗的、黑色的、深色的
n. 黑暗

反 義 bright adj. **明亮的**

例句

He has dark brown hair.
他有一頭深褐色的頭髮。

Some children are afraid of the dark.
有些小孩怕黑。

會話

A : It's too dark to read in the room.
房間裡光線太暗，以致於無法看書。

B : Why don't you turn on the light?
你為什麼不打開電燈？

A : Hey, you're shaking.
嘿，你在發抖耶！

B : I'm afraid of the dark.
我怕黑。

each

[itʃ]
adj. 每個的、各自的
adv. 各個地
pron. 每個（物品）、每人、每件（事）

例句

We said goodbye to each other.
我們互相道別。

She cut the cake into pieces and gave one to each of them.
她把蛋糕切成塊，給他們每人一塊。

會話

A : How much is it?
賣多少錢？

B : One hundred each.
每一個一百（元）。

A : What are their decisions?
他們的決定是什麼？

B : They each want to do something different.
他們各自都想做一些不同的事情。

every

['ɛvrɪ]

adj. 每一的、每個的、每隔…的、充分的

例句

I believe every word he says.
我相信他說的每一句話。

I always visit my parents every two months.
我每隔二個月拜訪我的雙親一次。

會話

A : Is the library open today?
圖書館今天有開館嗎？

B : The library is open every day.
圖書館每天都有開館。

A : What shall I do?
我應該怎麼辦？

B : You have every reason to try it once more.
你有充分的理由再試一次。

both

[boθ]
adj. 兩個的、一雙的
adv. 兩者、一雙
pron. 兩者、雙方

例句

They're both friendly.
他們兩人都很友善。

Susan and David both like dancing.
蘇珊和大衛兩人都喜歡跳舞。

會話

A : Do you know his parents?
你認識他的雙親嗎？

B : No, I don't know both his parents.
不認識，他的雙親我都不認識。

A : How was he?
他還好嗎？

B : No. Both his eyes were severely burned.
不好！他的雙眼都嚴重燒傷了。

far

[far]
adj. 遠的
adv. 遠地

反義 near adj. 近的

例句

Shall we walk? It's not far.
我們用走的好嗎？路不遠。

He was on the far side of the street.
他在街道的另一邊。

會話

A : Where is the post office?
郵局在哪裡？

B : It's far away from here.
離這裡很遠。

A : Do you know any other farms?
你知道還有其他農場嗎？

B : The farther farm is ten miles away.
更遠的農場在十英里之外。

fast

[fæst]
adj. 快的、迅速的、(鐘錶)偏快的
adv. 快地、迅速地

反 義 slow adj. adv. **緩慢的**

例句

They like fast music.
他們喜歡節奏快的音樂。

He ran faster and faster.
他越跑越快。

會話

A : What time is it?
現在幾點鐘?

B : It's ten o'clock. My watch is three minutes fast.
十點鐘。我的錶快了三分鐘。

fine

[faɪn]
adj. 很好的、健康的、美好的、晴朗的

類 似 nice adj. **美好的**

例句

We've a fine house.
我們擁有一棟漂亮的房子。

I take exercise in the fine morning.
我在晴天的早上做運動。

會話

A : Hi. How are you?
嗨！你好嗎？

B : Fine, thank you, and you?
很好啊，謝謝，你呢？

A : It's a fine day, isn't it?
天氣很好，對吧？

B : Yeah, it is.
是啊，的確是。

good

[gʊd]
adj. 良好的、令人滿意的、愉快的、漂亮的

同 義 great adj. 好的

例句

She's a good dancer.
她是一位傑出的舞者。

Did you have a good time?
你玩得開心嗎？

會話

A : How do you do?
你好嗎？

B : Good. How about you?
很好。你呢？

A : It's good to meet you.
真高興見到你。

B : Great to meet you, too.
我也很高興見到你。

excellent

['ɛksḷənt]

adj. 極好的、優秀的

同 義 wonderful adj. 極佳的

例句

He's excellent in mathematics.

他精通數學。

She is well known as an excellent singer.

她以身為一名優秀的歌手而聞名。

會話

A : Is David a singer?

大衛是歌手嗎？

B : No. he's not. He's an excellent composer and pianist.

不，他不是。他是一位優秀的作曲家和鋼琴演奏家。

A : What do you think of this hotel?

你覺得這家飯店如何？

B : Both the food and the service are excellent in this hotel.

這家旅館的食物和服務都非常好。

[bæd]

adj. 壞的、嚴重的

反 義 good adj. 良好的

例句

I have got a bad cold.

我得了重感冒。

He is a bad boy.

他是一個壞男孩。

會話

A : How is the weather out there?

外面天氣如何？

B : It's bad.

很糟！

glad

[glæd]
adj. 高興的、樂意的

同 義 happy adj. 快樂的

例句

I'm glad that he's got the job.
我很高興他得到了那份工作。

I'll be glad to do it for you.
我很樂意為你做這件事。

會話

A : Glad to meet you.
很高興認識你。

B : Me, too.
我也是。

A : I'm going to get married next month.
我下個月要結婚。

B : I'm glad to hear that.
真高興知道這件事。

exciting

[ɪk'saɪtɪŋ]
adj. 令人興奮的、使人激動的

例句

His days at the office were filled with important and exciting events.
他在辦公室工作的那些日子充滿了重要和令人激奮的事。

會話

A : He told us an exciting story.
他告訴了我們一個很刺激的故事。
B : What's it about?
有關什麼？

A : Did you have fun?
玩得開心嗎？
B : Yes, it's so exciting.
好玩，很刺激！

sad

[sæd]
adj. 悲傷的、糟透了的、暗淡的

反 義 happy adj. **快樂的**

例句

They are still sad about the dog's death.
他們還在為那條小狗的死而難過。

Don't be sad.
別難過了。

會話

A : My wife had a car accident last night.
我太太昨晚發生車禍了。

B : Don't be so sad.
別這麼難過了。

A : I felt sad.
我覺得傷心。

B : What's wrong? It's about John again?
怎麼啦？又是有關約翰的事嗎？

sorry

['sɔrɪ]

adj. 難過的、對不起、遺憾的

例句

I'm sorry to have kept you waiting so long.
對不起，讓你久等了。

I feel sorry for that elderly woman.
我為那位老太太感到難過。

會話

A : May I speak to John?
我可以和約翰講電話嗎？

B : I'm sorry, but he's on another line.
抱歉，但是他正在忙線中。

A : Sorry for that.
對於那件事真是抱歉！

B : That's OK. It won't bother me.
沒關係。不會造成我的困擾的。

cold

[kold]
adj. 冷的、寒冷的、冷淡的
n. 寒冷、著涼、感冒

反 義 hot adj. 熱的、炎熱的

例句

It's so cold outside.
外面很冷。

Be careful not to catch a cold.
小心別感冒了！

會話

A : You look terrible.
你看起來糟透了！

B : I have got a cold.
我感冒了！

A : How is the weather out there?
外面天氣如何？

B : It's pretty cold.
很冷喔！

sick

[sɪk]

adj. 生病的、有病的、厭惡的、對…厭煩的、噁心的

同義 ill adj. 生病的

例句

He has been sick for one week.
他已病了一個星期了。

I'm sick and tired of hearing it.
那件事我厭煩了，也聽膩了。

會話

A : You know what? I'm sick of you.
你知道嗎？我對你煩死了！

B : How could you say that?
你怎麼能這麼說？

A : Look at this, buddy.
兄弟，看這個！

B : Wow, I'm going to get sick.
哇，好噁心！

late

[let]

adj. 遲的、深夜的、已故的

adv. 晚地、遲地、黃昏地

反義 early adj. adv. 早的、提早的

例句

The train was 10 minutes late.
火車晚了 10 分鐘。

Tom was late for school.
湯姆上學遲到了。

會話

A : When did you get home?
你們什麼時候到家的？

B : We got home very late.
我們很晚才到家。

early

['ɝlɪ]
adj. 早的、早熟的
adv. 早地、提早地

反 義 late adv. adj. 晚的、遲的

例句

Is it still early?
還很早嗎？

The train was 10 minutes early.
火車早到十分鐘。

會話

A : Hurry up, we're late.
快一點，我們遲到了。

B : It's still early, isn't it?
還很早，不是嗎？

A : I'd like to see Mr. Jones.
我要見瓊斯先生。

B : You're early.
你早到了。

long

[lɔŋ]
adj. 〔距離、時間〕長的、長久的、長形的
adv. 長久地

反 義 short adj. 短的

例句

How long was her speech?
她的演講有多長的時間？

He hasn't long been back.
他才回來不久。

會話

A : Hurry up.
快一點！

B : I can't walk any longer.
我走不動了。

A : What the hell are you doing here?
你在這裡搞什麼？

B : It's a long story.
說來話長。

tall

[tɔl]
adj. 高的、大的、誇大的

反 義 short adj. 矮的

例句

Is the building tall?
那棟建築物很高嗎？

There are some tall buildings on Maple Street.
在楓葉街有一些高樓大廈。

會話

A : Is he tall?
他高嗎？

B : Yes, he's seven feet tall.
是啊，他有 7 呎高。

A : How tall is he?
他有多高？

B : Well, I'm not so sure.
嗯，我不太清楚！

short

[ʃɔrt]
adj. 矮的、短的、短暫的、缺乏的

反 義 tall adj. 高的

例句

He is a short man.
他是矮個子的人。

I'm short of money this week.
這個星期我的錢不夠用。

會話

A : How tall is he?
他有多高？

B : Pretty short.
非常矮。

A : Is he a tall guy?
他是個高個子的傢伙嗎？

B : No. He's a short white man.
不是。他是個矮個子的白人男性。

new

[nju]
adj. 新的、新鮮的

反 義 old adj. 舊的

例句

Have you seen her new car?
你有看過她的新車嗎？

Today I saw many new students.
今天我見到了許多新生。

會話

A : Your coat is worn out.
你的外套好破舊。

B : Yeah, I really need to get a new one.
是啊，我真的需要再買一件新的。

A : What a fashionable hat. Where did you get it?
好流行的一頂帽子。哪裡買的？

B : My father bought me as a birthday present.
我父親買來送我的生日禮物。

old

[old]
adj. 年老的、舊的、古老的

反義 young adj. 年輕的

例句

How old are you?
你多大年紀了？

There is an old bridge near my home.
我家附近有一座古老的橋。

會話

A : How old is your son?
你兒子多大年紀？

B : He's five years old.
他五歲。

A : Did you see an old lady around here?
你有看見附近有一位老太太嗎？

B : No, I didn't.
沒有，我沒有看見。

next

[nɛkst]
adj. 其次的、緊接著的
adv. 接著、然後、下一步
pron. 下一個

例句

What is your next plan?
你下一個計畫是什麼？

I'll tell you the answer when we next meet.
我們下一次見面時，我會把答案告訴你。

會話

A : If I miss this train I'll catch the next one.
如果趕不上這班火車，我會改搭乘下一班。

B : OK. I'll let you go now.
好吧！你先走吧！

only

['onlɪ]

adj. 唯一的、僅有的

adv. 只、僅僅、只是

例句

John is the only person who wants the job.
約翰是唯一想得到那份工作的人。

I saw him only yesterday.
我昨天才見到他的。

會話

A : Only five minutes left.
只剩下五分鐘了。

B : I'm late.
我遲到了！

A : Do you take credit cards?
你們收信用卡嗎？

B : Cash only.
只收現金。

rich

[rɪtʃ]
adj. 有錢的、含量豐富的、肥沃的

反 義 poor adj. 貧窮的

例句

He is a rich man.
他是一個有錢人。

This fish is rich in oil.
這種魚含脂肪很多。

會話

A : Do you like it?
你喜歡嗎？

B : No, I don't like rich food.
不，我不喜歡油膩的食物。

A : They're richer than anyone you'll ever meet.
他們將會是你見過比任何人還有錢的人。

B : No kidding.
不會吧！

poor

[pur]

adj. 貧窮的、可憐的、不好的、缺少的

例句

My English is poor.
我的英語不好。

He's such a poor person.
他真是可憐的人。

會話

A : What happened to the poor guy?
那個可憐的傢伙發生什麼事了？

B : He'd lost both his sons in the war.
他在戰爭中失去了僅有的兩個兒子。

A : Poor baby, where is your mom?
可憐的孩子，你媽咪在哪裡？

B : I don't know.
我不知道。

ready

['rɛdɪ]

adj. 準備好的、隨時待命的

例句

Are you ready?
你準備好了嗎？

The letters are ready for the post.
信件已準備好要寄了。

會話

A : Shall we?
可以走了嗎？

B : I'm ready. Let's go.
我準備好了。走吧！

A : I'm not ready for this.
這件事我還沒準備好。

B : Come on, sweetie, face it.
得了吧，甜心，面對它吧！

same

[sem]
adj. 同一的、同樣的
pron. 同樣的人（或事、物）

反義 different adj. 不同的

例句

They began to laugh at the same time.
他們同時笑了起來。

All the newspapers say the same.
所有的報紙登載的都一樣。

會話

A : How do you think of it?
你覺得如何？

B : It's all the same to me.
對我來說都是一樣的。

A : Merry Christmas.
耶誕快樂！

B : Same to you.
你也是。

different

['dɪfərənt]

adj. 不同的、有差異的

反 義 same adj. 相同的

例句

Different students go to different schools.
不同的學生上不同的學校。

A goat is different from a sheep.
山羊和綿羊是不同的。

會話

A : They're different, right?
他們是不同的，對吧？

B : I can't tell the difference between them.
我分不出來他們有什麼不同。

A : You're not like your sister.
你不像你的姊妹。

B : Of course not. We have different personalities.
當然不像。我們有不同的人格。

some

[sʌm]
adj. 某個、若干、一些、好幾個
pron. 一些、若干、有些人（或事、物）

例句

There must be some reasons for what he did.
他所做的事想必是有原因的。
Some of those stories are very good.
那些故事中有些是非常棒的。

會話

A : Something wrong?
有問題嗎？
B : Can't you hear that?
你沒聽到嗎？

A : I have some work to do tonight.
我今晚有工作要做。
B : Sure. Call me when you finish it.
好吧。做完後打電話給我吧！

many

['mɛnɪ]
adj. 許多的
pron. 許多人（或事、物）

例句

There are too many people here.
這裡的人太多了！

Now many people are learning computer.
現在有許多人在學電腦。

會話

A : Many things have to be done.
有許多事情需要做。

B : Sorry, I made a mistake.
抱歉，我弄錯了。

A : How many would you like?
你要幾個？

B : Five, please.
請給我五個。

few

[fju]
adj. 不多（的）、少數（的）
pron. 少數的人（或事、物）

例句

She has very few friends.
她的朋友非常少。

So few came that we were not able to hold the meeting.
人數太少，所以我們無法開成會。

會話

A : Hurry up! There are few minutes left.
快點！沒有幾分鐘了！

B : Don't worry, there are still a few minutes left.
別著急！還有剩幾分鐘的時間呢！

A : He has few good friends, right?
他幾乎沒有好朋友，是嗎？

B : I don't think so.
我不這麼認為。

important

[ɪm'pɔrtn̩t]
adj. 重要的、重大的、地位高的

例句

It is important to learn how to communicate.
學會如何溝通是很重要的。

He is an important official in the government.
他是政府的要員。

會話

A : Do you know how important it is?
你知道這有多重要嗎？

B : I don't think so.
我不這麼認為。

A : Is it really important?
這真的很重要嗎？

B : Yeah, it is important to me.
是的，對我來說是重要的。

strong

[strɔŋ]
adj. 強壯的、堅強的、濃烈的

反 義 weak adj. 弱的、虛弱的

例句

She is not very strong after her illness.
她病後身體不太好。

He has a strong will.
他有堅強的意志。

會話

A : I'd prefer some strong tea.
我要濃一點的茶。

B : Sure, here you are.
好的，請用。

A : Is he strong?
他強壯嗎？

B : No, he's a small guy.
不，他是個小個子。

wrong

[rɔŋ]
adj. 不對的、錯誤的、不適合的、有問題的

反 義 right adj. 對的、正確的

例句

There's something wrong with my head.
我的頭不太對勁。

I'm sorry I've got a wrong address.
對不起，我把地址弄錯了。

會話

A : What's wrong with you?
你怎麼啦？

B : I've a bad headache.
我的頭很痛。

A : Does anyone know where the post office is?
有人知道郵局在哪裡嗎？

B : You took the wrong way.
你走錯路了！

right

[raɪt]

n. 右、右邊

adj. 右邊的、正確的

adv. 向右地、正確地、完全地

反義 left n. adj. adv. 左、左面、向左

例句

Is that the right time?
那是正確的時間嗎？

Turn right at the crossing.
在十字路口向右轉。

會話

A : How should I do it?
我應該怎麼做？

B : Go right back to the beginning.
直接回到開始處。

A : It's on your right side.
在你的右手邊。

B : I see. Thank you.
我瞭解了！謝謝你。

angry

['æŋgrɪ]

adj. n. 憤怒的、生氣的、因為…而生氣

同 義 mad adj. 發怒的、生氣的

例句

She often gets angry about trivial things.
她常因瑣碎小事而發火。

Don't be angry with me for not having written.
別因為我沒有寫信而生我的氣。

會話

A : Are you OK? You look so angry.
你還好吧？你看起來好生氣。

B : David stood me up last night.
大衛昨天晚上放我鴿子。

A : Don't be so angry, pal.
伙伴，不要這麼生氣！

B : But he drove me crazy.
但是他把我搞瘋了！

another

[ə'nʌðɚ]

adj. 再一、另一、別的、不同的

pron. 另一個、再一個

例句

That's another matter.
那是另外一回事。

He lost his pen and borrowed one from another boy.
他的筆弄丟了，就從別的男孩那兒借了一支。

會話

A : Would you like to have dinner with me?
你要和我一起用晚餐嗎？

B : I'd love to, but I have another plan.
我很希望去，但是我有其他計畫了。

A : How can you do this to him?
你怎麼能夠這樣對待他？

B : Do you have another solution?
你還有其他解決的辦法嗎？

other

['ʌðɚ]
adj.（兩者中）另一個的、其餘的、更多的
pron.（兩個中的）另一個人（或物）、其餘的人（或物）、另一方

例句

It is hard to tell the twin brothers one from the other.
這對孿生兄弟很難辨認。

Is there any other kind?
還有其他種類嗎？

會話

A : Sorry, I have other plans.
抱歉，我有其他計畫。

B : That's OK. Maybe some other time.
沒關係。也許改天。

A : There are other ways to do this exercise.
還可以用別的方法做這個練習。

B : You show me.
你做給我看啊！

familiar

[fə'mɪljɚ]
adj. 熟悉的、隨便的、通曉…

例句

Her name is familiar to all of us.
她的名字為我們大家所熟知。

會話

A : You look familiar.
你看起來好眼熟。

B : You too. Are you Tony from Taiwan?
你也是。你是來自台灣的東尼嗎？

A : Do you know how to solve this question?
你知道要如何解決這個問題嗎？

B : Sure. I'm familiar with it.
當然知道！我很熟悉這件事。

famous

['feməs]
adj. 著名的、有名的

例句

France is famous for its fine food and wine.
法國以精美的食物和葡萄酒而聞名。

A famous movie star has come to live in our town.
一位有名的電影明星到我們城裏來生活了。

會話

A : Is he a singer?
他是歌手嗎？

B : You don't know anything about him? He's a famous singer.
你完全不知道他的事嗎？他是位有名的歌手。

NEW BASIC
VOCABULARY
1000

CHAPTER 03 動詞篇

TRACK 3

do

[du]
v. aux. 做（事）
(p. pp. =did; done)

相 關 does（do 的第三人稱單數現在式）

例句

I'll do my best to do my work well.
我會盡力做好我的工作。
How do you do?
你好嗎？

會話

A : Aren't you going to do something different?
你不想點不同的辦法嗎？
B : What can I do?
我能做什麼？

A : Did you do your homework?
你有做功課嗎？
B : Yes, I did.
有的，我有做。

can

[kæn]
v. aux. 能、會、可以、可能
(p. =could)

例句

She can speak French.
她會說法語。

You can't play football here.
你不能在這裡踢足球。

會話

A : Can you do me a favor?
你可以幫我一個忙嗎？

B : Sure. What is it?
當然可以。什麼事？

A : Can you remind me that eating crap makes me feel like crap?
你可以提醒我，吃垃圾食物讓我感覺像是垃圾嗎？

B : Sure, no problem.
當然好，沒問題。

may

[me]
v. aux. 可以、也許、可能、祝、願

例句

May I come in?
我可以進來嗎？

May you succeed!
祝你成功！

會話

A : May I help you?
要我幫忙嗎？

B : Yes. May I take a look at it?
是的。我可以看一下這個嗎？

A : What's your plan?
你的計畫是什麼？

B : We may go out to eat.
我們也許可以出去吃。

[wɪl]

v. aux. 將…、意思、主觀促成、遺贈

例句

They say it will rain tomorrow.
他們說明天會下雨。

He willed his house to his son
他立下遺囑，把房子留給兒子。

會話

A : Will you call him again, please?
可以請你再打電話給他嗎？

B : OK, I will.
好的，我會的。

A : You will come, won't you?
你會過來，對吧？

B : Maybe. I don't know for sure.
可能會！我不確定。

must

[mʌst]
v. aux. 必須、必定是

例句

I must leave at six today.
我必須在今天六點鐘離開。
You mustn't tell anyone about this.
這件事你不能告訴任何人。

會話

A : What happened to John?
約翰怎麼啦？
B : I don't know. He must have read the letter.
我不知道。他一定已經看過那封信了。

A : I must leave now.
我現在要走了。
B : OK. Catch you later.
好啊！再見囉！

go

[go]
v. 去、走、通到、達到
（p. pp. =went; gone）

相 關 goes（go 的第三人稱單數現在式）

例句

It's late; I must go.
時間不早了，我必須走了。

We went to France for our holidays.
我們到法國去度假。

會話

A : Which road goes to the station?
哪一條路通向車站？

B : That way.
那一個方向。

A : Where would you like to go?
你要去哪裡？

B : I'd like to go to the museum.
我要去博物館。

come

[kʌm]
v. 來、來到
(p. pp.=came; come)

反義 go v. 去

例句

The train came slowly into the station.
火車緩緩駛進車站了。

Where do you come from?
你是哪裡人？

會話

A : Where are you from?
你來自哪裡？

B : I came here from Japan.
我來自日本。

A : Here comes my bus. See you later!
我的公車來了。再見囉！

B : See you soon.
再見！

want

[want]

v. 要、想要、必要、需要

例句

Somebody wants to see you.
有人想見你。

What you want is a holiday.
你所想要的是休假。

會話

A : What do you want for your birthday?
你生日想要什麼禮物？

B : I want a bicycle.
我想要一部腳踏車。

A : Do you want another drink?
你要再來喝一杯嗎？

B : Sure, why not?
好啊，為什麼不要？

hand

[hænd]

v. 送、遞給、交付

n. 手、(鐘錶)指針

例句

He handed me a glass of beer.
他遞給我一杯啤酒。

It was written by hand.
這是手寫的。

會話

A : Please hand me the book.
請把書遞給我。

B : Here you are.
給你。

A : Where is it exactly?
正確位置究竟在哪裡?

B : It's on your right hand.
在你的右手邊。

have

[hæv]
v. 有、吃、喝、得到
(p. pp. =had; had)

例句

Do you have a pencil?
你有鉛筆嗎？

I had the news from John.
我從約翰那裡得知這個消息。

會話

A : Have some tea.
喝些茶吧！

B : Thanks a lot.
多謝啦！

A : What do you want to have?
你想要吃什麼？

B : I'd like to have a sandwich.
我想要吃三明治。

get

[gɛt]
v. 獲得、成為、到達
(p. pp.=got; got 或 gotten)

例句

How did you get the money?
你是如何弄到這筆錢的？

When did you get back?
你什麼時候回來的？

會話

A : It's getting dark.
天漸漸黑了。

B : Come on, let's go home.
走吧，我們回家吧！

A : Could you get me a Diet Coke?
請給我低卡可樂好嗎？

B : OK. I'll be right back with you.
好的！馬上來。

give

[gɪv]
v. 給予、付出、舉辦、獻出
(p. pp. =gave; given)

例句

We'll give a welcome party on Monday afternoon.
我們將在週一下午舉行歡迎會。

The doctor told me to give up smoking.
醫生要我戒煙。

會話

A : Give me the bags while you open the door.
你開門時把那些包包給我。

B : Here you are.
給你。

A : I'd like to give him another chance.
我想再給他另一次機會。

B : I don't agree with you.
我不同意。

make

[mek]

v. 做、製造、使得、料理

(p. pp. =made; made)

例句

The chairs were made of wood.
椅子是用木頭製造的。

Some paper is made from bamboo.
有的紙是竹子做的。

會話

A : Will you make me some coffee, please?
可以請你幫我煮咖啡嗎？

B : No problem.
沒問題。

A : Make sure the door is shut on your way out, OK?
確定你出去的時候門要關上，好嗎？

B : No problem.
沒問題。

happen

['hæpən]
v. 碰巧、偶然發生

例句

We happened to be in the neighborhood.
我們正好在附近。

It so happened that I saw him yesterday.
我昨天碰巧看見他了。

會話

A : When did the explosion happen?
爆炸是什麼時候發生的？

B : Last night, I guess.
我猜是昨天晚上。

A : If I were you, I'd hang around. See what happens.
如果我是你，我會在附近閒晃。看看什麼事會發生。

B : That's what you'd do?
你會這麼做嗎？

change

[tʃendʒ]
v. 改變、更換、兌換、換穿衣物
n. 改變、更換、零錢

例句

If you want, you can change seats with me.
如果你願意，你可以和我交換座位。
We changed the date to September 17th.
我們將日期改為九月十七日。

會話

A : Where is Maria?
瑪麗亞人呢？
B : She went upstairs to change her clothes.
她上樓去換衣服了。

A : Do you have any change?
你有零錢嗎？
B : No. I have no small change.
沒有。我沒有零錢。

cause

[kɔz]

v. 引起、使發生

n. 原因、起因、理由

例句

The cause of the fire was carelessness.
起火的原因是因為疏忽。

Don't stay away without cause.
不要無故缺席。

會話

A : You've caused trouble to all of us.
你給我們大家都添了麻煩。

B : I'm really sorry.
我真的很抱歉。

A : I didn't know what had caused him to change his mind.
我不知道是什麼原因促使他改變主意。

B : Maybe it's because of his mother.
也許是因為他的媽媽（的緣故）。

know

[no]

v. 知道、認識、懂得、辨別

(p. pp. =knew; known)

例句

I know him to be an honest man.

我知道他是一位誠實的人。

I knew it is true.

我就知道那是事實。

會話

A : How long have you known David?

你認識大衛有多久了？

B : I've known him for years.

我認識他好幾年了。

A : You know Charles, right?

你認識查爾斯，對吧？

B : No, but...

不認識，但是…

hear

[hɪr]

v. 聽見、聽說、得知

(p. pp. =heard; heard)

例句

I haven't heard from John.
最近我都沒有約翰的消息。

I listened but heard nothing.
我有仔細聽，但什麼也沒聽到。

會話

A : I've heard a lot about you.
久仰大名！

B : Nothing bad, I hope.
希望不是壞事。

A : What did you hear?
你聽到什麼？

B : Someone was crying.
有人在哭。

listen

[ˈlɪsn̩]
v. 仔細聽、傾聽

例句

I listen to the radio every day.
我每天都聽收音機。

I didn't listen to what he was saying.
我沒注意聽他在講什麼。

會話

A : Listen. Do you hear that?
聽。你有聽見嗎？

B : What's wrong?
怎麼啦？

A : Listen, I've been thinking.
聽著，我想了好久。

B : Yeah?
什麼事？

say

[se]
v. 說、講、據說
(p. pp. =said; said)

例句

So I said to myself, I wonder what she means.
因此我想，我不知道她是什麼意思。

He is said to be rich.
據說他很有錢。

會話

A : How much did you say?
你說（賣）多少錢？

B : It's five thousand dollars.
五千元。

A : Say, I was wondering, would you like to come over?
這麼說吧，我在想，你願意過來嗎？

B : Sorry, I'm afraid not.
抱歉，恐怕不行。

speak

[spik]
v. 說話、說（某種語言）
（p. pp. =spoke; spoken）

例句

I'd like to speak to you about my idea.
我想和你談談我的想法。

I was so surprised that I could hardly speak.
我驚訝得說不出話來。

會話

A : May I speak to Kenny?
我可以和肯尼說話嗎？

B : Wait a moment, please.
請稍等。

A : Speaking of David, where is he?
說到大衛，他（人）在哪裡？

B : I haven't seen him for a long time.
我好久沒見到他了。

talk

[tɔk]
v. n. 說、講、聊天、告知

例句

Tell me the truth, did you talk to him?
告訴我實話，你有和他說話嗎？

She had a long talk with her daughter.
她和女兒作了一次長談。

會話

A : I'd like to talk to you about something.
我有點事要和你談。

B : What is it?
什麼事？

A : We've got to talk.
我們需要談一談。

B : Wait a moment, please.
請稍等。

tell

[tɛl]
v. 告訴、命令、區分
(p. pp.=told; told)

例句

Do you think children should do as they're told?
你認為孩子們應按照吩咐行事嗎？
It's difficult for us to tell the difference between the two cats.
要我們區別這兩隻貓是很困難的事。

會話

A : I've told you not to be there, right?
我有告訴過你不要過去那裡，對吧？
B : I'm sorry, sir.
抱歉，長官。

A : Let me tell you something about marriage.
讓我告訴你什麼是婚姻。
B : What's the point?
你要說的重點是什麼？

see

[si]

v. 看、注意、理解、拜訪

(p. pp.=saw; seen)

例句

I saw him going into the station.
我看著他走進了火車站。

Did you see where I had put my glasses?
你有看到我把眼鏡放在哪裡了嗎？

會話

A : I can't see why you don't like him.
我不明白你為什麼不喜歡他。

B : Because he's a jerk.
因為他是個混蛋。

A : I haven't seen you for so long.
好久不見！

B : What have you been up to?
你都去哪裡啦？

watch

[watʃ]
v. 觀看、注視、看守
n. 手錶、懷錶、小心、看守

例句

They watched the car go past.
他們看著汽車開過去了。

I've lost my watch.
我把我的手錶弄丟了。

會話

A : Do you often watch TV?
你經常看電視嗎？
B : Yes, I do.
是的，我經常看。

A : What out.
小心！
B : What? What's wrong?
什麼？怎麼啦？

look

[lʊk]

v. 觀看、注意、好像、顯得、朝著

n. 觀看、臉色、外表

例句

You look tired.
你看起來很累！

Let me have a look at the lovely puppy.
讓我看一下那隻可愛的小狗。

會話

A : What are you looking for?
你在找什麼？

B : My textbook. I can't find it.
我的課本。我找不到。

A : It's freezing today, isn't it?
今天真冷啊，對吧！

B : Yeah, you look warm all bundled up like that.
是啊！你裹得那樣看起來很暖和。

send

[sɛnd]
v. 送、寄出、派遣、傳遞、迫使
(p. pp. =sent; sent)

反 義 receive v. **收到**

例句

He was sent by his mother to buy some milk.
他母親叫他去買牛奶。

Some people were sent to help them.
有一些人被派出去幫助他們。

會話

A : If you need money I'll send it to you.
如果你需要錢，我會送過去給你。

B : It's very kind of you.
你真好心！

A : Why did you send me flowers?
你為什麼要送花給我？

B : I wanted you to know that somebody loved you.
我想要你知道，有人愛著你。

deliver

[dɪ'lɪvɚ]
v. 遞送、交付、發言

同 義 send v. **遞送**

例句

The newspapers will be delivered in five hours.
這些報紙將於五小時內送達。

The postman's job is to deliver letters and parcels.
郵差的工作是投遞信件和包裹。

會話

A : Would you deliver this box to Jim?
可以把這個箱子送給吉姆嗎？

B : As you wish.
悉聽尊便。

A : I'll deliver a speech at the meeting tomorrow morning.
明天上午我要在會議上發表演說。

B : What are you going to say?
你要說什麼？

hold

[hold]
v. 拿著、握住、舉行
(p. pp.=held; held)

例句

She held little Jenny in her arms.
她抱著小珍妮。

Could you hold on? I'll just see if he's in.
你不要掛斷好嗎？我去看一看他在不在。

會話

A : When did you have the meeting?
你們什麼時候開會的？

B : We held the meeting on Tuesday.
我們星期二舉行了會議。

A : I'd like to talk to George.
我要和喬治講電話。

B : Hold on a second, please.
請稍等！

depend

[dɪ'pɛnd]
v. 依靠、相信、依賴

例句

Whether the game will be played depends on the weather.
球賽是否要舉行，要視天氣而定。

Good health depends upon good food, exercise and getting enough sleep.
良好的健康要靠良好的食物、運動和充分的睡眠。

會話

A : When do you leave for Japan?
你什麼時候要去日本？

B : It depends on the weather.
視天氣而定。

A : I knew he wasn't to be depended upon.
我就知道他不可信賴。

B : Then why did you call him?
那麼你為什麼又打電話給他？

desire

[dɪ'zaɪr]
v. 要求、期望
n. 欲望、要求

例句

Everybody in the world desires peace and happiness.
全世界所有的人都渴望和平和幸福。

It's impossible to satisfy all their desires.
使所有人的欲望都得到滿足是不可能的。

會話

A : I desire to go home to have a look.
我很想回家去看一看。

B : Yeah, you really should go home this summer.
是啊，你這個夏天真的應該要回家。

A : I desire to see you at once.
我想立刻和你見面。

B : But I don't want to see you now.
但是我現在不想見到你。

read

[rid]
v. 讀、朗讀、察覺
(p. pp. =read [rɛd])

例句

They are learning to read.
他們在學朗讀。

We read English aloud every morning.
我們每天早上都大聲地朗讀英語。

會話

A : What are you doing now?
你現在在做什麼？

B : I'm reading newspaper.
我正在讀報紙。

A : She read my thoughts.
她看出了我的心思。

B : But you just met her last week.
但是你上週才認識她的。

study

['stʌdɪ]

v. 學習、研究、細看

n. 學習、研究、調查、學問

同義 learn v. 學習

例句

They studied many ways to get there.
他們研究了很多去那裡的辦法。

How are you getting along with your studies?
你的研究進展得怎麼樣？

會話

A : What's your plan tonight?
你今晚的計畫是什麼？

B : I'll have to study English.
我要讀英語。

A : What do you study?
你在學什麼？

B : I study Chinese with him.
我和他一起學中文。

teach

[tiʧ]
v. 教、教書
(p. pp. =taught; taught)

反義 learn v. 學習

例句

David teaches my son history.
大衛教我兒子歷史。

He taught the boys how to play football.
他教這些男孩們學習踢足球。

會話

A : How did you learn it?
你怎麼學會的？

B : My father taught me.
我父親教我的。

A : Would you teach me English?
你可以教我英文嗎？

B : No problem.
沒問題！

write

[raɪt]

v. 書寫、寫信、填寫、寫下

(p. pp. =wrote; written)

例句

I wrote some letters last night.
昨晚我寫了幾封信。

He has written some good stories.
他已經寫了一些好的小說。

會話

A : Please write down what you hear.
請寫下你聽到的內容。

B : No problem, sir.
沒問題的，先生。

A : How often do you write your parents?
你多久寫信給你的父母？

B : I write to them once a month.
我每個月寫一次信給他們。

draw

[drɔ]
v. 畫、繪製、拉、拖、牽
(p. pp. =drew; drawn)

同 義 pull v. 拉、拖

例句

Jenny draws very well.
珍妮畫得很好。

He drew the chair toward her.
他把椅子拉向她。

會話

A : What did you draw, Michael?
麥克，你畫什麼？

B : I drew a house.
我畫了一棟房子。

A : Would you please draw a chair for me?
可以幫我拉一張椅子嗎？

B : No problem.
沒問題！

work

[wɝk]
v. n. 工作、勞動、運轉

例句

I've been working in the garden all afternoon.
我整個下午一直在花園裡工作。

I'm taking some work home from the office.
我要從辦公室帶點工作回家做。

會話

A : Don't work too hard.
不要工作得太辛苦。

B : I won't.
我不會的。

A : Don't you think you should work out?
你不覺得你應該要運動嗎？

B : But I have no time.
但是我沒時間啊！

worry

['wɝɪ]

v. 煩惱、憂慮

例句

My toothache worries me a great deal.
我的牙疼使我很煩惱。

He's worried about his son.
他為兒子而煩惱。

會話

A : Don't worry about him. He's OK.
不要擔心他。他沒問題的。

B : You think so?
你是這麼認為的嗎？

A : David, you've changed. I'm really worried about you.
大衛，你變了。我真的很擔心你。

B : Come on, I'm fine.
不要這樣，我很好的。

accept

[ək'sɛpt]
v. 接受、領受、認可

例句

We must accept the fact that we have lost the chance.
我們必須承認這個事實，那就是我們已經失去了這次機會。

I received his present yesterday, but I didn't want to accept it.
我昨天收到了他的禮物，但是我並不想接受。

會話

A : I asked her to marry me. She accepted.
我向她求婚。她答應了。

B : I'm glad to hear that.
我很高興聽見這個消息。

A : I should accept his offer.
我應該接受他的提議。

B : What makes you think so?
你為什麼會這樣認為？

act

[ækt]
v. 表演、扮演、演出
n. 表演、法令、行為

相關 actor n. 男演員 actress n. 女演員

例句

Helping a blind man is an act of kindness.
幫助盲人是慈善的行為。

A trained dog can act as a guide to a blind person.
一條受過專門訓練的狗可以充當盲人的嚮導。

會話

A : He acts the part of Romeo.
他扮演羅密歐這個角色。

B : I think he acted his part well.
我覺得他把角色演得不錯。

add

[æd]

v. 加、增加上、補充說明

例句

His illness added to our difficulties.
他的病增加了我們的困難。

"I felt sorry for her," added Bob.
「我為她感到惋惜。」鮑伯又說道。

會話

A : What is the total?
總共是多少？

B : It's twenty. Because five and fifteen add up to twenty.
是二十。因為五加十五是二十。

A : The fire is going out. Will you add some wood?
火就要滅了，你加一些木頭好嗎？

B : No problem.
好的！

admit

[əd'mɪt]

v. 承認（＋doing）、允許進入、接納

例句

Two hundred children are admitted to our school every year.
我們學校每年錄取 200 名兒童。

Tom was put in prison. He admitted that he had been on the march.
湯姆被抓進監獄。他承認參加了遊行。

會話

A : He admitted having read the letter.
他承認看過那封信。

B : Really? I can't believe it.
真的？真不敢相信！

A : Come on, admit it. You're a loser.
得了吧，承認吧！你是一個失敗者。

B : But I don't want to.
但是我不想要（承認）。

advise

[əd'vaɪz]

v. 忠告、勸告、勸說、通知、建議

同義 recommend v. 建議

例句

The doctor advised him to have a complete rest.

醫生勸告他要完全休息。

They advised the old man to give up smoking.

他們勸告那個老人戒煙。

會話

A : I advised her that she should wait.

我勸她要等。

B : Why don't you just pick her up?

你為什麼不乾脆去接她？

A : What did the doctor say?

醫生說什麼？

B : He advised me to do exercise.

他建議我做運動。

afford

[ə'fɔrd]
v. 擔負得起（……的費用）、抽得出（時間）、提供

例句

I can't afford to pay such a price.
我付不起這個價錢。

I can't afford to do this.
我無法做這件事。

會話

A : How about this one?
這個你覺得如何？

B : I can't afford to buy this coat.
我買不起這件外套。

A : I'm not sure I could afford the time.
我不確定是否抽得出時間。

B : Come on. That would be fun.
來嘛！會很好玩的。

believe

[bɪ'liv]
v. 相信、信仰、認為

同 義 trust v. 相信

例句

I can't believe you easily.
我不能輕易相信你。
You'll never believe what I did.
你不會相信我做了什麼事。

會話

A : How can you make me believe you?
你該怎麼讓我相信你呢？
B : Believe me. I'm telling the truth.
相信我。我說的是實話。

A : We believe going for a run every morning to be good for health.
我們認為每天早上跑步對健康有益。
B : I agree with you.
我同意。

agree

[ə'gri]

v. 同意、贊同、一致、適合

反 義 disagree v. 不同意

例句

I agree with every word you've said.
我同意你說的每一句話。

He agreed to get someone to help us.
他同意找人來幫我們的忙。

會話

A : What do you think?
你覺得呢？

B : I totally agree to his proposal.
我完全同意他的計畫。

A : We agreed on a date for the next meeting.
我們就下次會議的日期達成了協定。

B : But I don't agree with you on many things.
但是在很多事情上，我和你的意見有分歧。

discuss

[dɪ'skʌs]

v. 討論、商議、詳述

例句

We discussed what to do and where we should go.
我們討論了該做什麼事和該去什麼地方。

The committee discussed the matter from all conceivable angles.
委員會從各種角度討論了那件事。

會話

A : I have something of great importance to discuss with you.
我有十分重要的事情要和你討論。

B : What can I do for you?
我能幫你什麼忙?

A : I refused to discuss the matter.
我拒絕討論這件事。

B : But I really need your advice.
但是我真的需要你的建議。

argue

['argjʊ]
v. 爭吵、爭辯

例句

We're always arguing about money.
我們總是為錢爭吵。

What are you two arguing about?
你們兩個到底在爭辯什麼？

會話

A : But it's not fair, is it?
但是不公平啊，對吧？

B : Do what you are told and don't argue with me.
叫你怎麼做，你就怎麼做，不要和我爭論。

A : I'm not going to argue with you tonight.
今晚我不想和你爭吵。

B : Neither am I.
我也不想。

bear

[bɛr]
v. 忍受、容忍
(p. pp. =bore; borne)
n. 熊

例句

She bore the pain with great courage.
她以極大勇氣忍受著痛苦。

Bears hibernate during the winter.
熊在冬季冬眠。

會話

A : I can't bear that fellow.
我忍受不了那個傢伙。

B : Come on. He didn't mean it.
好了拉！他沒有惡意。

A : I couldn't bear it anymore.
我再也聽不下去了。

B : Neither could I.
我也聽不下去。

beat

[bit]

v. （連續地）打、敲、拍、（心臟）跳動、戰勝
(p. pp.=beat; beaten)

例句

The police beat the door down in order to get into the house.
警察連續敲門想要進去房子裏。

She beat her brother at tennis.
她打網球勝過她兄弟。

會話

A : What did you hear?
你聽見什麼？

B : Only its heart beating.
只有它的心臟跳動聲。

A : What do you wish?
你許什麼願望？

B : I hope to beat the record.
我希望能打破記錄。

beg

[bɛg]
v. 乞求、請求
(p. pp. ppr.=begged; begged; begging)

例句

He's begging for money from the people in the street.
他在街上向人要錢。

She begged me not to tell her parents.
她請求我不要告訴她的父母。

會話

A : May I beg you to open the window?
請你把窗戶打開好嗎？

B : No problem.
沒問題！

A : I beg your pardon?
你說什麼？

B : I said I'd like to talk to Jennifer.
我說我要和珍妮佛講電話。

slow

[slo]
v. 放慢
adj. 慢的、緩慢的
adv. 緩慢地

反 義 hurry v. 加快

例句

The bus was so slow that I was late for school.
公共汽車開太慢，使我上學遲到了。

John ran slower than the others.
約翰比其他人跑得慢。

會話

A : Slow down, boy.
慢一點，年輕人。

B : Don't call me boy.
不要叫我年輕人。

A : Is it fast enough?
夠快嗎？

B : No, it's too slow.
不，太慢了。

hurry

['hɝɪ]

v. n. 趕緊、急忙

例句

Don't hurry, we're not late.
不用急，我們還不算晚。

Don't drive so fast, there is no hurry.
不要把車開得這麼快，沒有必要急急忙忙。

會話

A : Hurry up. We're late.
快一點！我們遲到了。

B : OK, OK.
好，好！

A : What's the rush?
急急忙忙要去哪裡？

B : I was in a hurry to go home.
我急著要趕回家。

smile

[smaɪl]
v. n. 微笑

例句

He smiled at me.
他向我微笑。

She couldn't remember anything but his gentle smile.
除了他紳士般的微笑，她什麼也記不住了。

會話

A : What are you smiling at?
你在笑什麼？
B : Nothing.
沒事啊！

A : You look different.
你看起來不太一樣喔！
B : You know what? Maria smiled at me this morning.
你知道嗎？瑪麗亞今天早上對我笑。

laugh

[læf]

v. 笑、嘲笑

n. 笑、笑聲、使人發笑的事

例句

It was so funny; I couldn't stop laughing.
事情這麼有趣，逗得我大笑不止。

The king was laughed at by everybody.
國王受到所有人的嘲笑。

會話

A : They always laugh at me.
他們總是嘲笑我。

B : Come on, it's no big deal.
不要這樣嘛，沒什麼了不起的！

A : Why are you laughing?
你為什麼在笑？

B : I'm not laughing. I'm crying.
我沒在笑。我在哭。

cry

[kraɪ]

v. 喊叫、哭

n. 叫喊、哭聲

例句

The little boy cried out with pain.
這個小男孩疼得大叫。

We heard the cry of a bear.
我們聽到熊的吼聲。

會話

A : Hey, stop crying.
嘿，不要哭了！

B : But I can't help it.
但是我情不自禁！

A : What's that noise?
那是什麼吵鬧聲音？

B : A girl is crying for help.
一個女孩子在大聲呼救。

help

[hɛlp]

v. 幫助、援助、補救、避免

n. 幫助、助手、有幫助的人

例句

Would you help me carry the heavy bag?
你能幫我提一下那個重的袋子嗎？

I couldn't help laughing.
我忍不住要笑。

會話

A : Would you help me, please?
可以請你幫我嗎？

B : Sure, what is it?
好啊，什麼事？

A : Can you help me?
你可以幫我嗎？

B : No. You have to help yourself.
不要！你要靠自己。

live

[lɪv]
v. 居住、活、生存

反義 die v. 死亡

例句

The Chinese live on rice.
中國人以米為主食。

My grandmother lived to be eighty.
我的祖母活到八十歲。

會話

A : Where do you live?
你住哪裡？

B : I live in Taipei.
我住在台北。

A : Do you live with your parents?
你和父母一起住嗎？

B : Yes, I do.
是的，我是。

die

[daɪ]

v. 死、滅亡、渴望

(p. pp. ppr. =died; died; dying)

例句

He's born in 1980 and died in 2004.
他生於 1980 年，死於 2004 年。

My grandfather died 6 years ago.
我爺爺六年前去世了。

會話

A : When did he die exactly?
他到底什麼時候死的？

B : He died in 1999.
他 1999 年過世的。

love

[lʌv]
v. 愛、愛戴、喜好、想要
n. 熱愛、愛情、很喜歡、喜愛的事物

反義 hate v. 討厭、恨

例句

I like him but I don't love him.
我喜歡他，但我並不愛他。

He has a strong love for his mother.
他深深愛著自己的母親。

會話

A : What happened to you?
你怎麼啦？

B : Nothing, I just don't love him anymore.
沒事，我只是不再愛他了。

A : You are gonna love this.
你一定會喜歡這個的。

B : I'm dying to hear it.
我倒很想聽聽。

like

[laɪk]
v. 喜歡、想要、願意
prep. 像、跟…一樣

反 義 dislike v. 不喜歡

例句

I like to go to school by bike.
我喜歡騎自行車去上學。

Do like this.
照這樣做。

會話

A : I'd like to speak to David.
我要和大衛講電話。

B : Hold on a second, please.
請稍等。

A : Which one would you like, the red one or the blue one?
你喜歡哪個，紅的還是藍的？

B : The red one.
這個紅色的。

forget

[fə'gɛt]
v. 忘記、忘掉、忘記帶（或買）、放棄
(p. pp. =forgot; forgotten)

反 義 remember v. **記得**

例句

Forget it.
算了吧！

I'll never forget meeting you for the first time.
我永遠忘不了和你初次見面的情景。

會話

A : Don't forget to meet her at six.
別忘了六點鐘要和她見面。

B : I won't.
我不會（忘記）的。

A : One more thing I forgot to mention is that I was broke.
還有一件事我忘了提起 ： 我破產了。

B : How did this happen?
怎麼發生的？

remember

[rɪ'mɛmbɚ]
v. 記得、想起、回憶起、記住、代…問好

同 義 recall v. 記得、回憶起

例句

I can't remember how to get there.
我想不起是怎麼到那裡的。

I remember posting it.
我記得我寄了。

會話

A : Remember to send my letter.
記得替我把信寄出去。
B : I will.
我會的。

A : Remember how we said that someday we'd move to New York?
記得我們說過有一天我們要搬到紐約嗎？
B : So what?
那又怎麼樣？

leave

[liv]
v. 離開、把…留下、委託
(p. pp.=left; left)

例句

I hope they'll leave soon.
我希望他們趕快離開。

When do you leave for Taiwan?
你什麼時候要去台灣？

會話

A : What did he say?
他說什麼？

B : Nothing. He just left a letter for us.
沒事。他只有留一封信給我們。

A : Would you like to leave a message?
你要留言嗎？

B : Sure. Tell Mr. Jones to return my call.
好啊！告訴瓊斯先生回我電話。

let

[lɛt]
v. 讓、允許
(p. pp. =let; let)

例句

She lets her children play in the street.
她讓她的孩子在街上玩。

Let us go to help that elderly man, will you?
讓我們去幫助那個老人，你說好不好？

會話

A : Let's go to the cinema.
我們去看電影。

B : What do you want to see?
你想看什麼？

A : Let me hold this cup for you.
我幫你拿著杯子。

B : Thanks.
多謝啦！

lie

[laɪ]

v. 躺臥、平放、位於

(p. pp. ppr.=lay; lain; lying)

例句

The book is lying on the table.
這書本放在桌上。

I lay down on the grass.
我躺在草地上。

會話

A : I feel awful.
我覺得糟透了。

B : You should lie down.
你應該躺下來。

find

[faɪnd]

v. 找到、發現、發現處於某種狀態

（p. pp.=found; found）

例句

I can't find my shoes.

我找不到我的鞋子。

When I woke up, I found myself in hospital.

我醒來時，發覺自己在醫院裡。

會話

A : Did you find anything you like?

找到喜歡的東西了嗎？

B : Yes, show me that blue tie, please.

是的，請給我看那條藍色領帶。

A : I couldn't find the key.

我找不到鑰匙。

B : Has someone got it?

有人拿走了嗎？

meet

[mit]

v. 碰見、遇見

(p. pp.=met; met)

例句

I met Henry in the street yesterday.
昨天我在街上遇到亨利。

If you come, I'll meet you at the station.
如果你要來，我會到車站去接你。

會話

A : How do you meet David?
你怎麼認識大衛的？

B : We went to the same high school.
我們是高中同學。

A : I'm glad to meet you.
真高興認識你。

B : It's my pleasure.
我的榮幸。

feel

[fil]
v. 觸摸、感覺、覺得
(p. pp.=felt; felt)

例句

The doctor felt my arm to find out if it was broken.
醫生摸摸我的手臂，看看是否斷了。

I don't feel like sleeping.
我不想睡覺。

會話

A : Would you feel like a cup of coffee?
你要喝咖啡嗎？

B : OK. Thanks.
好啊！謝謝！

A : I felt very happy.
我覺得很幸福。

B : I'm so glad to hear that.
我很高興知道這件事。

miss

[mɪs]

v. 想念、思念、錯過、未擊中

n. 未中、達不到

例句

I'll miss you.

我會想念你的。

He ran fast but missed the bus.

他跑得很快，但還是錯過了公共汽車。

會話

A : Just go straight ahead?

只要往前直走？

B : Yeah. It's on the right. You won't miss it.

是啊！就在右邊。你不會看不見的。

A : I miss you.

我想念你。

B : I miss you, too.

我也想念你。

hope

[hop]
v. 希望、期望
n. 希望、盼望、期望、被寄託希望的人或物

同義 wish v. n. **希望、盼望**

例句

I hope it'll be sunny tomorrow.
希望明天是個晴天。

He didn't give up his hope.
他並沒有放棄他的希望。

會話

A : What's your trip plan?
你的旅遊計畫是什麼？

B : I hope to visit Japan this year.
我希望今年能到日本訪問。

A : What do you hope?
你希望什麼？

B : I wish I had a boyfriend.
我希望我有男友。

call

[kɔl]

v. n. 稱呼、打電話、呼喚、拜訪、命名

同 義 shout v. **呼喊、大聲說**

例句

We'll call the baby Joan.
我們會給嬰兒取名瓊。

I'll call you at six.
我六點鐘會打電話給你。

會話

A : Could I call on you on Sunday?
我星期天可以去拜訪你嗎？

B : Sure, anytime on Sunday.
當然可以，星期天任何時間都可以。

A : Call me sometime, huh?
有空打電話給我，好嗎？

B : I will.
我會的。

answer

['ænsɚ]
v. 回答、答覆、接（電話）、應（門）
n. 回答、答覆、回信、答案

同義 reply v. 回答、答覆

例句

Could you answer the riddle, please?
請你解開這個謎好嗎？

What's your answer, David?
大衛，你的答案是什麼？

會話

A : What are you doing now?
你現在正在做什麼？

B : I'm waiting for an answer to my letter.
我正在等候回信。

A : Isn't he answering your phone?
他沒有接你的電話嗎？

B : He must be gone.
他一定是離開了。

buy

[baɪ]
v. 購買（p. pp. =bought; bought）
n. 購買、便宜貨

反 義 sell v. 販售

例句

Father bought me a car as a present of my birthday.
爸爸給我買了一輛車作為我的生日禮物。

It's a good buy.
買得真便宜。

會話

A : Are you looking for something special?
你在找什麼特別的東西嗎？

B : I'll buy my wife a watch.
我要買一支錶給我的太太。

A : Did he buy you anything?
他有買任何東西給你嗎？

B : Not really.
不算有！

enjoy

[ɪn'dʒɔɪ]
v. 喜歡、享有、欣賞

例句

I enjoyed the film.
我很喜歡看這部電影。

I hope you're enjoying your staying here.
希望你在這裡過得愉快。

會話

A : Did you enjoy yourself tonight?
你今晚玩得開心嗎？

B : Yes, I did. Thanks for inviting me.
是的，我玩得很開心。謝謝你邀請我。

A : How do you think of Taiwan?
你覺得台灣怎麼樣？

B : I enjoyed the days in Taiwan.
我在台灣的這一段日子很開心。

eat

[it]
v. 吃、食
(p. pp.=ate; eaten)

例句

We eat up all the sweets and fruit.
我們吃光所有的糖果和水果。

What did you eat for lunch?
你午餐吃了什麼？

會話

A : What would you like to eat?
你想吃什麼？

B : How about Chinese food?
中國料理怎麼樣？

A : What would you want?
你想吃什麼？

B : I'd like to eat an apple.
我想要吃蘋果。

drink

[drɪŋk]

v.　喝、飲、喝酒 (p. pp. =drank; drunk)

n. 飲料、酒〔常用複數〕

例句

Drink your tea before it gets cold.
把茶喝了，別讓它涼了。

I like soft drinks.
我愛喝不含酒精的飲料。

會話

A : What would you like to drink?
你想要喝什麼飲料？

B : Tea, please.
請給我茶。

A : Do you have any cold drinks?
你們有冷飲嗎？

B : Sure, what do you want to have?
當然有，你想喝什麼？

need

[nid]
v. n. 需要、必要

例句

The doctor told me that I needed a good rest.
醫生告訴我必須好好休息。

會話

A : I feel terrible.
我覺得糟透了。

B : You need to get some sleep.
你需要睡一下。

A : I figured you'd need one of these.
我猜你會需要一個這個。

B : Thanks. It's very kind of you.
多謝！你真好心。

dry

[draɪ]
v. 使…乾燥
adj. 乾燥的、乾的

例句

It's getting dry.
快乾了。

Please dry the dish with the towel.
請用這條毛巾把盤子擦乾。

會話

A : Do you have any dry mushrooms?
你們有賣乾燥的香菇嗎？

B : Here you are.
在這裡。

bring

[brɪŋ]
v. 帶來、拿來
(p. pp.=brought; brought)

例句

Spring brings beautiful flowers.
春天帶來美麗的花朵。

Bring your homework tomorrow.
明天把你的家庭作業帶來。

會話

A : Anything else?
還需要其他東西嗎？

B : Just bring me a napkin.
只要幫我拿一條餐巾來。

A : What can I do for you?
需要我服務的嗎？

B : Can you bring me another frozen Magarita?
可以再幫我拿一些冰的瑪格麗特雞尾酒嗎？

take

[tek]

v. 拿、花費（時間）、吃喝（餐點、藥）、乘車（船）
(p. pp. =took; taken)

反義 bring v. 帶來

例句

Take this medicine after each meal.
每餐後服用此藥。

I'll take them to the zoo.
我要帶他們到動物園。

會話

A : Do you have any plans tomorrow?
你們明天有什麼計畫嗎？

B : Yes, I'll take them to the zoo.
有啊，我要帶他們到動物園。

A : Where did you go this afternoon?
你們今天下午去哪裡了？

B : I took Peter to the park.
我帶彼得去公園了。

borrow

['baro]
v.（向別人）借、借用

反義 lend v. **出借**

例句

Can I borrow your ruler?
我能借用你的尺嗎？

I borrowed eight hundred dollars from him.
我向他借了八百元。

會話

A : May I borrow your magazines?
我可以借你的雜誌嗎？

B : Sure. Go ahead.
當然好。拿去吧！

A : I was wondering if I could borrow some shampoo.
我在想我可以向你借一些洗髮精嗎？

B : Shampoo? Sure, here you are.
洗髮精？當然可以，給你。

begin

[bɪ'gɪn]

v. 開始、著手、創建、源於

(p. pp. ppr.=began; begun; beginning)

同 義 start v. 開始

例句

She began working for him in 2006.
她從 2006 年就開始替他工作。

I began to study at seven.
我七點鐘開始學習。

會話

A : When did you begin learning English?
你何時開始學英語的？

B : When I was thirteen years old.
當我十三歲的時候。

A : Will you begin to paint the fence now, please?
可以請你現在開始油漆圍籬了嗎？

B : But I'm still busy now.
可是我現在還在忙。

start

[start]

v. n. 開始、著手做、出發

反 義 finish v. **完成**

例句

It's a long trip; we'll have to start early.
路途很長，我們必須早點出發。

That's a good start.
那是一個好的開始。

會話

A : If everyone is ready, we can start.
如果每個人都準備好了，我們可以開始了。

B : I'm ready.
我準備好了。

A : Shall we start?
我們可以開始了嗎？

B : OK. Let's start.
可以！我們開始吧！

finish

['fɪnɪʃ]
v. 結束、做完

同 義 complete v. 完成

例句

What time does the concert finish?
音樂會何時結束？

I always have to stay up late to finish my homework.
我總是要熬夜到很晚把我的功課做完。

會話

A : I haven't finished reading that book yet.
我還沒有讀完那本書。

B : Why? It's already 10 o'clock.
為什麼？已經十點鐘了耶！

A : When shall I finish it?
我要什麼時候完成？

B : By 2 o'clock this afternoon.
今天下午兩點鐘之前。

stop

[stap]
v. 停止、阻止
(p. pp.=stopped; stopped)
n. 停止、車站

例句

You must stop her from telling such lies.
你必須阻止她撒這種謊言。

He stopped to smoke.
他不再抽菸。

會話

A : You should stop smoking.
你應該要戒煙。

B : I'm OK. Don't worry about me.
我很好。不用擔心我。

A : I'm going to get off at the next stop.
我要在下一站下車。

B : No problem.
沒問題！

become

[bɪ'kʌm]

v. 變得、成為

（p. pp. =became; become）

例句

She became a famous writer.
她成了有名的作家。

It's now become a rule in the country.
它現已成為該國的法規。

會話

A : How is it going now?
事情進行得如何了？

B : Well, it became complicated.
嗯，變得有點複雜了。

A : We became actual friends.
我們變成真正的朋友了。

B : You did? I can't believe it.
你們是嗎？我真不敢相信！

ask

[æsk]
v. 詢問、請求

例句

Ask him if he'd like a drink.
問他要不要喝一杯。

He asked to join our group.
他要求加入我們的團體。

會話

A : Can I ask you a question?
我能問你一個問題嗎？

B : Sure. What is it?
好啊！什麼事？

A : I have other plans. Thanks for asking, though.
我有其他計畫了。還是感謝你的邀請。

B : Maybe some other time.
也許改天吧！

keep

[kip]
v. 保持、保存、保留
(p. pp. =kept; kept)

例句

That will keep you busy for some time.
那會使你忙一陣子。

You can keep it; I don't need it.
你可以將它留下，我不需要了。

會話

A : Keep the change.
不用找零錢了！

B : Thank you.
謝謝你。

A : Keep in touch.
保持聯絡。

B : I will. Take care of yourself.
我會的！你要多保重！

cook

[kʊk]
v. 烹調、烹煮
n. 廚師

例句

I'm going to cook dinner tomorrow.
明天我要做晚飯。

My brother is a good cook.
我的哥哥是一個好廚師。

會話

A : Do you know how to cook onion soup?
你知道如何煮洋蔥湯嗎?

B : Of course I do.
當然知道。

A : Wanna come over and cook dinner for me?
想要來幫我煮晚餐嗎?

B : Uh, I can't.
嗯,我不行!

cut

[kʌt]
v. 切、剪、割、削
n. 刀傷、剪、割

例句

He cut his fingers on the broken glass.
他被碎玻璃割破了手指。

He had a cut on his face.
他的臉上有一道刀傷。

會話

A : What happened to you?
你怎麼啦？

B : I cut my hand on the broken glass.
我被破玻璃割破手。

A : Did you cut yourself?
你割傷你自己了嗎？

B : No, I didn't.
沒有，我沒有。

close

[kloz]
v. 關、閉
adj. 接近的、靠近的、親密的
adv. 靠近地

反 義 open v. adj. **打開**

例句

The shop has been closed though it is only 3 pm.
儘管才下午三點，這個商店已經關門了。

He followed close behind me last night because he felt so afraid.
由於害怕，昨天晚上他緊跟在我的後面。

會話

A : Who is that tall guy?
那個高個子的傢伙是誰？

B : He's David, my closest friend.
他是大衛，是我最親密的朋友。

A : Do you think we're close?
你認為我們親密嗎？

B : Sometimes. Why?
有的時候。為什麼（這麼問）？

open

['opən]
v. 打開、張開
adj. 開著的、開口的

同 義 shut v. 關上

例句

I've opened the door.
我已經打開了門了。
So the door is open now.
所以現在門是開著的。

會話

A : What did you do?
你做了什麼事？
B : I just opened the window a minute ago.
我一分鐘之前才把窗戶打開的。

A : Why don't you open the door on your way out?
你為什麼不出去的時候把門打開？
B : OK. I'll open the door.
好，我會打開門。

play

[ple]
v. 玩、打球、演奏樂器
n. 玩耍、戲劇

例句

They are playing games.
他們正在玩遊戲。

I like playing football.
我喜歡踢足球。

會話

A : Do you know how to play guitar?
你知道怎麼彈吉他嗎？

B : No, I don't.
不，我不會。

A : What did you do last night?
你們昨晚做了什麼事？

B : We went to see the play.
我們昨天去看戲了。

arrive

[ə'raɪv]
v. 到達、抵達

例句

What time does the plane arrive in New York?
飛機何時抵達紐約？

I arrived at the station at eight am.
我早上八點鐘抵達車站。

會話

A : When did you arrive here?
你什麼時候到達這裡的？

B : I've just arrived.
我才剛到。

A : Will we arrive in Taipei on time?
我們會準時抵達台北嗎？

B : I'm afraid not.
恐怕不行。

clean

[klin]
v. 弄乾淨、打掃
adj. 乾淨的、清潔的

例句

Please clean it up.
請清理乾淨。

We do some cleaning once a month.
我們每月做一次大掃除。

會話

A : Did you clean your room?
你有打掃房間嗎？

B : Yes, I did it last night.
是的，我昨晚就做了。

A : Did you wash your hands?
你有洗手嗎？

B : My hands are clean.
我的手很乾淨。

clear

[klɪr]
v. 澄清、清除、收拾
adj. 清楚的、明朗的

例句

This soap should help clear your skin.
這塊肥皂會幫助你把皮膚洗乾淨。

After the storm, the sky cleared.
暴風雨過後，天晴了。

會話

A : Let me clear off the plates.
我來把盤子收拾走。

B : Thanks.
謝謝！

A : It's clear from his actions that he loves her.
從他的行動明顯看出他是愛她的。

B : Are you sure?
你確定？

pay

[pe]

v. 付錢、給報酬、給予注意

n. 工資

例句

Pay attention to what I'm saying.
請注意我說的話。

He gets his pay each Thursday.
他每星期四領工資。

會話

A : I'll pay you $3 to clean my car.
我付你三元去清洗我的車。

B : Really?
真的？

A : How much should I pay?
我應該要付多少？

B : It's eight hundred.
八百（元）。

pull

[pʊl]
v. 拉、拖、拔〔瓶塞、牙齒等〕、牽
n. 拉、拖、拉力、把手

反義 push v. 推

例句

I couldn't pull the boat out of the water.
我無法把小船從水裡拉出來。

I had the bad tooth pulled out.
我讓人把那顆蛀牙拔了。

會話

A : Can you pull it for me?
你可以幫我拉一下嗎？

B : No problem.
沒問題！

A : It isn't heavy. I'll pull it.
這不重。我來拉。

B : Thank you so much.
非常感謝！

push

[pʊʃ]
v. 推、推進、逼迫
n. 推、擠、努力

例句

Please push the car!
請推一下這輛車！

I gave the window a push.
我推了那扇窗戶。

會話

A : How to use this machine?
要怎麼使用這部機器？

B : You can push the button like this one.
你可以像這樣按這個按鈕。

A : Push harder.
用力一點推。

B : Or what do you think I'm doing now?
不然你以為我現在在幹嘛？

put

[put]
v. 放、擺、裝、施加、寫上、穿衣
(p. pp. = put; put)

同義 place v. 放、擺

例句

Please put your shoes here.
請把你的鞋子放在這兒。

The bus put down three men.
公車讓三個人下了車。

會話

A : Don't forget to put on your coat.
不要忘記穿上你的外套。

B : OK.
好的。

A : Where did you put my bag?
你把我的袋子放在哪裡？

B : It's in your room.
在你的房間裡。

build

[bɪld]

v. 建築、造、建設

(p. pp. =built; built)

例句

When was the house built?
這棟房子是什麼時候建造的？

We have built a lot of tall buildings.
我們已建造了許多高樓。

會話

A : What did you build, Ted?
泰德，你蓋了什麼？

B : This is a castle.
這是一個城堡。

A : What did you do this summer vacation?
你們這個暑假作了什麼事？

B : We built a house for our mother.
我們替我們的母親蓋了一間房子。

save

[sev]
v. 挽救、節省、儲蓄

反 義 waste v. 浪費

例句

She saved her friend from falling.
她救了她的朋友，没有讓她掉下去。

You have saved me 10 dollars.
你替我省了 10 元。

會話

A : It'll save you a lot of time.
它會幫你省很多時間。

B : Thank you for telling me.
謝謝你告訴我。

A : I saved a lot of money.
我存了很多錢。

B : You did?
是嗎？

thank

[θæŋk]

v. n. 感謝、謝謝

例句

The old lady thanked me for helping her.
這個老太太感謝我幫了她。

He sent me a letter of thanks.
他寫了一封感謝函給我。

會話

A : It's on your right side. You won't miss it.
在你的右邊。你不會看不見的。

B : Thank you so much.
非常感謝你。

A : Thanks. It's very kind of you.
謝啦！你真好。

B : Don't mention it.
不客氣！

welcome

['wɛlkəm]
v. n. adj. 歡迎

例句

Welcome home.
歡迎回來！

Welcome to Taipei!
歡迎光臨台北！

會話

A : Thank you.
謝謝你。

B : You are welcome.
不客氣！

A : Welcome to Taiwan.
歡迎光臨台灣。

B : I'm so happy to be here again.
我真高興又來這裡了。

think

[θɪŋk]
v. 想、思考、認為
(p. pp.=thought; thought)

例句

Think hard before you answer the question.
回答問題前先仔細想一想。

Well, you should think it over.
嗯！你應該好好想想這件事。

會話

A : What do you think about it?
你覺得呢？

B : Well, it's a good chance.
嗯，是個好機會。

A : Would you like to go to see a movie with me?
你要和我去看電影嗎？

B : Um, I really don't think I can.
嗯，我想我無法去耶！

expect

[ɪk'spɛkt]
v. 盼望、認為

類 似 hope v. 希望

例句

We expected that you would wait for us here.
我們還以為你會在這裡等我們呢！
We were expecting a letter from her at that time.
我們當時正在等待著她的來信。

會話

A : I'd like to meet Mr. Jones.
我要見瓊斯先生。
B : Mr. Jones is expecting you.
瓊斯先生正在等你來。

A : Don't worry about him.
不用擔心他。
B : What else do you expect?
不然你還期望什麼？

face

[fes]
v. 面向、面對
n. 臉部

例句

I couldn't face another day at work, so I pretended to be sick.
這工作我一天也面對不了，因此我假裝生病。

It was hard to keep a straight face while I answered their questions.
回答他們的問題時，我很難忍住不笑。

會話

A : I don't want to admit my failure.
我不想承認我的失敗。

B : Come on, you've got to face it.
得了吧，你必須要面對它。

A : Why did he say so?
他為什麼這麼說？

B : Because he didn't want to lose face.
因為他不想丟面子。

carry

['kærɪ]

v. 提、扛、搬、運送、攜帶

(p. pp. ppr.=carried; carried; carrying)

類 似 bring v. 攜帶

例句

Can you carry the heavy box?
你搬得動這個重箱子嗎？

I carried a basket in my hand.
我手裏拎著籃子。

會話

A : Who is going to carry this box?
誰要拿這個盒子？

B : It's Johnny.
是強尼。

A : Can you carry this for me?
可以幫我搬這個嗎？

B : No problem.
沒問題！

catch

[kætʃ]
v. 抓住、接住、捕獲、趕上（車輛）、患病
（p. pp. = caught; caught）

例句

The dog caught the ball in its mouth.
狗用嘴咬住了球。

I'm going to catch the train.
我要去趕搭火車。

會話

A : You walk on and I'll catch up with you later.
你往前走，我等一會兒會趕上你的。

B : OK, hurry up.
好，要快一點。

A : You'll catch a cold if you don't put a coat on.
如果你不穿上外套會感冒的。

B : All right, mom.
好的，媽咪。

try

[traɪ]

v. 嘗試、努力、試驗

(p. pp. ppr.=tried; tried; trying)

例句

I don't think I can do it very well, but I'll try my best.
我認為自己做不好，但我會盡力的。

This malady tries me so much.
這個疾病把我折磨得好慘。

會話

A : Why don't you get some sleep?
你怎麼不試著睡一下？

B : I've tried it. But it didn't help.
我試過了。但是一點幫助都沒有。

A : There you are. I've been trying to reach you.
你來了。我一直試著聯絡你。

B : I'm always here.
我都在這裡啊！

turn

[tɝn]
v. 旋轉、轉動、轉變

例句

She turned the key in the lock.
她把鑰匙塞進鎖裡轉動了一下。

Please turn to page 10.
請翻到第十頁。

會話

A : Please turn on the radio.
請打開收音機。

B : No problem.
沒問題！

A : Would you turn off the light?
你可以關燈嗎？

B : Sure.
當然好！

use

[juz]
v. 使用、應用、慣常（＋ to）

例句

We use a computer to do all its accounts.
我們用電腦來計算所有帳目。

I used to live in Taipei.
我過去一向住在台北。

會話

A : How do you use it?
你怎麼使用它的？

B : Let me show you.
我來示範給你看。

A : I really hate it.
我真的很討厭這件事。

B : Don't worry, kid. You'll get used to it.
孩子，不要擔心。你會習慣的。

visit

['vɪzɪt]

v. n. 參觀、訪問、拜訪

例句

When we were in London, we visited the Tower twice.
在倫敦期間，我們參觀了倫敦鐵塔兩次。

I paid my first visit to New York yesterday.
我昨天第一次到紐約旅遊。

會話

A : Do you have any plans tomorrow?
你明天有事嗎？

B : I'll visit my folks in the country.
我要去鄉下探望我的父母。

A : Can I visit you this weekend?
我這個週末可以去拜訪你嗎？

B : You're always welcome.
歡迎！

wait

[wet]
v. 等候、等待

相關 waiter n. 男侍者 waitress n. 女侍者

例句

We waited 20 minutes for a bus.
我們等公車等了二十分鐘。

Could you wait for me for a while?
你能等我一會兒嗎？

會話

A : May I speak to David?
我可以和大衛說話嗎？

B : Yes. Wait a moment, please.
好的。請稍等。

A : What are you waiting for?
你在等什麼？

B : What do you think I'm waiting for?
你覺得我在等什麼？

dress

[drɛs]
v. 穿衣、穿著
n. 服裝、女服、童裝

例句

She's dressing her baby.
她正在幫她的嬰兒穿衣服。

Try on this dress, please.
請試穿這件衣服。

會話

A : Hurry up. We're late.
快一點！我們遲到了！

B : I'll be ready in a moment; I'm dressing.
我一會兒就好，我正在穿衣服。

A : Do we have to wear evening dress for this party?
我們是不是必須穿晚禮服去參加這次的派對？

B : Of course.
當然（需要）！

drive

[draɪv]

v. 駕駛、駕車、驅趕、迫使

(p. pp.=drove; driven)

例句

She drives well.

她的駕駛技術很好。

The farmer was driving his cow along the road.

農夫趕著他的母牛沿著那條路走去。

會話

A : Let me drive you home this evening.

今晚讓我開車送你回家吧！

B : Thanks, David. It's very nice of you.

大衛，謝謝你。你真是好心！

A : Everything about him began to drive me crazy.

有關他的所有事開始讓我發瘋。

B : Come on, you've got to relax.

好了啦，你需要放輕鬆！

break

[brek]
v.　割、打破、違反、摔斷、打碎
(p. pp. =broke; broken)

例句

The bottle fell on the floor and broke.
瓶子掉到地板上並破了。

The bank was broken into yesterday.
銀行昨天被闖入。

會話

A : What happened?
發生什麼事了？

B : My car has broken down.
我的汽車壞了！

A : Are you OK?
你還好吧？

B : I had my leg broken yesterday.
昨天我把腿摔斷了。

brush

[brʌʃ]
v. 刷、擦
n. 刷子（pl. brushes）

例句

We should brush our teeth everyday.
我們應該每天刷牙。

The toothbrush should be changed once a month.
牙刷應該一個月更換一次。

會話

A : Did you brush your teeth this morning, Johnny?
強尼，你今天早上有刷牙嗎？

B : Yes, I did.
是的，我有。

A : How often do you brush your teeth?
你有多經常刷牙？

B : I brush my teeth everyday.
我每天刷牙。

fish

[fɪʃ]
n. 魚、魚肉
v. 捕魚、釣魚

例句

We had some fish for dinner.
我們晚餐吃了一些魚。

We caught three little fishes.
我們捉了三條小魚。

會話

A : Let's go fishing now.
我們現在去釣魚吧！

B : Sure.
好啊！

walk

[wɔk]
v. 走過、沿…走、遛狗
n. 步行、走、散步

例句

She likes walking.
她喜歡散步。

I usually take a walk after supper.
我通常在晚飯後散步。

會話

A : Is it far from here?
離這裡很遠嗎？

B : It's just a ten minutes' walk.
走路只要十分鐘。

A : Would you walk my dog, please?
可以請你遛我的狗嗎？

B : Why me again?
為什麼又是我？

stand

[stænd]
v. 站、站起、忍受
(p. pp. =stood; stood)

反義 sit v. 坐

例句

I couldn't get a seat on the bus, so I had to stand.
我在公車上找不到位子，因此只好站著。

I can't stand being in the same room with him.
我不能忍受和他待在同一個房間中。

會話

A : Stand up, please.
請站起來。

B : Why? What's wrong?
為什麼？有問題嗎？

A : I just can't stand him.
我就是受不了他！

B : But he's your husband.
但是他是你的丈夫啊！

sit

[sɪt]

v. 坐、位於

(p. pp. ppr. =sat; sat; sitting)

例句

He sat at his desk working.
他坐在書桌前工作。

Sit down please, children.
孩子們，請坐下。

會話

A : Can I talk to you now?
我現在能和你說話嗎？

B : Sure. Sit down.
當然可以。坐下吧！

A : May I sit down here?
我能坐在這裡嗎？

B : Sorry, it's taken.
抱歉，（這裡）有人坐。

sleep

[slip]
v. 睡覺、與…上床（發生性關係）
(p. pp.=slept; slept)
n. 睡眠、睡眠時間

例句

She slept a good sleep.
她睡了個好覺。

I haven't had enough sleep.
我睡眠不足。

會話

A : Did you sleep with her?
你有和她發生關係嗎？

B : No! No! No! I just kissed her.
沒有！沒有！沒有！我只有吻她而已。

A : I'm home.
我回來了！

B : Are you OK? Do you want to get some sleep?
你還好吧？你想要睡一下嗎？

run

[rʌn]

v. 行駛、競選、奔跑、趕緊、逃跑
(p. pp. ppr.=ran; run; running)

n. 跑、奔跑

例句

The school is a ten minutes' run from the bank.
從銀行到學校跑步需要十分鐘。

I ran into an old friend in a pub.
我在酒吧碰到了一位老朋友。

會話

A : Will he run for Governor?
他會競選州長嗎？

B : He will.
他會的。

A : I've got to run some errands.
我要去辦一些事。

B : I'll go with you.
我和你一起去。

jump

[dʒʌmp]
v. n. 跳、跳躍

例句

She jumped out of the window.
她跳出窗外。

He got the first in the long jump.
他跳遠得了第一名。

會話

A : Who jumped the highest?
誰跳得最高？

B : I did.
是我（跳得最高）。

NEW BASIC VOCABULARY 1000

CHAPTER 04
副詞篇

TRACK 4

about

[ə'baʊt]
adv. 到處、大約
prep. 關於、在各處

例句

It took me about five minutes to find the book.
找那本書花了我大約五分鐘的時間。

How about going shopping?
要不要去購物？

會話

A : How are you doing?
你好嗎？

B : Great. How about you?
不錯！你呢？

A : Oooh, poor baby.
可憐的寶貝！

B : Hey, what are you saying? I'm not your baby.
嘿，你說什麼？我不是你的寶貝。

after

['æftɚ]
adv. 後來、以後
conj. 在…以後

反義 before adv. conj. 之前

例句

David came last Tuesday, and I came the day after.
大衛上星期二來，我則是次日來的。

I found your coat after you'd left the house.
在你離開屋子後我找到了你的外衣。

會話

A : What did you do after school?
放學後你做了什麼？

B : Nothing much.
沒什麼事！

A : Why don't you give her a call after she got home?
你為什麼不在她到家後打電話給她？

B : I just don't want to.
我就是不想要。

before

[bɪ'for]
adv. 以前
conj. 在…之前

例句

I've never seen the film before.
我以前從沒看過這部電影。

I drank a glass of milk before I went to bed.
我睡覺前喝了一杯牛奶。

會話

A : Have you ever been to Japan before?
你以前有去過日本嗎？

B : No, I haven't.
沒有，我沒去過。

A : Have you two met before?
你們兩人以前見過面嗎？

B : I'm afraid not.
恐怕沒有（見過面）。

ago

[ə'go]
adv. 以前、(自今)…前

例句

He left five minutes ago.
他五分鐘前就離開了。

I saw him two years ago.
我兩年前見過他。

會話

A : When did your grandfather die?
你祖父什麼時候過世的?

B : He died many years ago.
他好多年前過世的。

A : Have you ever met him before?
你以前見過他嗎?

B : Yes, we went to the same school 2 years ago.
有的,我們兩年前是同學。

already

[ɔl'rɛdɪ]
adv. 已經、早已

例句

I've seen the movie already.
我已經看過這部電影了。
I have finished it already !
我都已經做完了！

會話

A : Are you going to join me?
你要加入我嗎？
B : I'd love to. But I've already got plans.
我是很想。但是我已經有計畫了。

A : I've seen that TV show already.
我已經看過那個電視節目了。
B : When? Why didn't you tell me?
什麼時候的事？你為什麼沒有告訴我？

always

['ɔlwez]
adv. 總是、一直、永遠、始終

例句

They always make fun of me.
他們總是嘲笑我。

He isn't always friendly.
他不是個友善的人。

會話

A : What do you usually do in the morning?
你早上通常在做什麼？

B : I always check my e-mail.
我總是在收發我的電子郵件。

A : Why didn't you invite him?
你為什麼不邀請他？

B : Because he's always mean to me.
因為他總是對我很壞。

away

[ə'we]
adv. 不在、離…之遠

反 義 near adv. 近的

例句

Jenny is away from home.
珍妮不在家。

The post office is only two blocks away.
郵局（距離這裡）只有兩個街道遠。

會話

A : Has David come back yet?
大衛回來了嗎？

B : No, he is still away.
沒有，他還是不在。

A : Is the bank close to the school?
銀行離學校很近嗎？

B : No, it is not. It's far away from the school.
不，沒有。它離學校很遠。

back

[bæk]
adv. 向後、回原處
adj. 背面的、反面的
n. 背後、後面

例句

Put it back when you've finished it.
當你完成時，要放回去。

Someone patted me on the back.
有人在我背上輕輕地拍了一下。

會話

A : Don't look back.
不要向後看。

B : Why not? What's wrong?
為什麼不要？怎麼啦？

A : Where are you going?
你要去哪裡？

B : I'll be back in a minute.
我馬上回來。

down

[daʊn]
adv. 向下、往下、倒下
prep. 沿著（街道、河流）向下

反義 up adv. conj. 往上

例句

They live just down the road.
他們就住在街的那一頭。

I want to go down town with you.
我想和你一起到市區去。

會話

A : Excuse me, where is the post office?
請問，郵局在哪裡？

B : Walk down the street and you'll see it on the right.
沿這條街往下走，你就會看到在右手邊。

A : Look down there.
往下看那裡！

B : Nothing down there.
下面沒東西啊！

here

[hɪr]
adv. 這裡、向這裡、這時
n. 這裡

反 義 there adv. n. **那裡**

例句

Come over here, please.
請到這裡來。

Here comes my bus.
我的公車來了。

會話

A : Where am I on the map?
我在這張地圖上的哪裡？

B : You are over here.
你在這裡。

A : Come over here, baby.
寶貝，過來。

B : OK, mom.
好的，媽咪。

there

[ðɛr]

adv. 在那兒、往那兒、在那方面、你看、有（與 be 動詞連用）

n. 那裡

例句

I live there.
我住在那裡。

Is there a telephone near here?
這附近有電話嗎？

會話

A : Are there any bigger ones?
有大一點的嗎？

B : Yes, we have some bigger ones.
有的，我們有大一點的。

A : Where did you put it?
你把它放在哪裡？

B : It's over there.
在那邊。

how

[hau]
adv. 多少、多麼地、如何

例句

How old are you?
你多大年紀？

How difficult the book is!
這是多難懂的一本書啊！

會話

A : How much does it cost?
這個值多少錢？

B : Five hundred dollars.
五百元。

A : Do you know how it happened?
你知道是怎麼發生的嗎？

B : I have no idea.
我不知道！

just

[dʒʌst]
adv. 正好、剛才、僅僅

例句

She was sitting just here.
她剛才就坐在這裡。

I don't want any dinner; just coffee.
我不想吃晚飯，只想喝點咖啡。

會話

A : I worry about him.
我真是擔心他。

B : Just relax, OK?
放輕鬆，好嗎？

A : Do you know where David is?
你知道大衛在哪裡嗎？

B : Nope. I have no idea. He just left.
不知道！我不知道！他剛離開。

maybe

['mebɪ]
adv. 大概、也許（表示可能性）

例句

Maybe we should tell him all the things.
也許我們應該告訴他所有的事。

Maybe you are right.
也許你是對的。

會話

A : Will they come?
他們會來嗎？

B : Maybe.
也許吧！

A : What are you going to do tonight?
你們今晚要做什麼？

B : Maybe we'll go to a party at a friend's house.
也許我們會去朋友家聚餐。

never

['nɛvɚ]

adv. 決不、從來沒有

例句

I've never met such a strange man.
我從沒碰到過這麼奇怪的人。

Never forget to lock the door at night.
晚上別忘了鎖門。

會話

A : Have you ever been to Japan?
你去過日本嗎？

B : Never.
從沒有！

A : How was the party?
派對好玩嗎？

B : I'll never go there again.
我再也不會去那裡了。

yes

[jɛs]
adv. 是、好、同意

反 義 no adv. 不、沒有

例句

A : Do you know him?
你認識他嗎？

B : Yes and no.
算是又不是。

會話

A : Don't you like cats?
你不喜歡貓嗎？

B : Yes, I do.
不，我喜歡。

A : Are you ready?
你準備好了嗎？

B : Yes, I am.
是的，準備好了。

not

[nat]
adv. 不、沒…

例句

Today is not Sunday.
今天不是星期天。

He is not so poor as his brother.
他不像他兄弟那樣窮。

會話

A : Sorry to bother you.
抱歉打擾你了！

B : It doesn't matter.
沒關係！

A : We're not friends any longer.
我們不再是朋友了！

B : What's the matter with you?
你怎麼啦？

now

[naʊ]
adv. 現在、此刻

例句

What time is it now?
現在幾點了？

I'm reading a book now.
我正在看一本書。

會話

A : Are you busy now?
你現在忙嗎？

B : Yeah, I'm busy with the projects.
是啊，我正在忙計畫案。

A : Go now or you'll be late.
你得馬上走，不然就要遲到了。

B : Hey, don't worry about me.
嘿，不用擔心我！

often

['ɔfən]

adv. 經常地、通常地

例句

She often has a headache.
她經常頭疼。

We often go finishing on weekends.
我們週末經常去釣魚。

會話

A : How often do you go there?
你隔多久去那裡一次？

B : Once a month.
每個月一次。

A : What did you do during your summer vacation?
你們暑假期間做了什麼事？

B : We often go hunting.
我們常常去打獵。

usually

['juʒʊəlɪ]
adv. 通常地、經常地

反 義 unusually adv. 不經常地

例句

He usually gets up early.
他經常很早起床。

I usually have a cup of coffee in the morning.
我早上通常會喝一杯咖啡。

會話

A : What do you usually do on weekends?
你們週末通常都在做什麼？

B : We usually go shopping.
我們通常去購物。

really

['rɪəlɪ]
adv. 真正地、確實地

例句

I really don't want anymore.
我真的不想再要了。

We really need your help.
我們真的需要你的幫忙。

會話

A : I've found a job.
我找到工作了。

B : Really?
真的嗎？

A : Did you wish you had someone to care of you?
你希望有一個人可以照顧你嗎？

B : Not really.
不盡然希望！

too

[tu]
adv. 也、太、過分

例句

Jack can speak French, too.
傑克也會說法語。

It's too cold to go swimming.
天氣太冷，不能去游泳。

會話

A : Help me with it.
幫幫我。

B : Hey, you're going too much.
嘿，你很過分喔！

A : It was nice talking to you.
很高興和你聊天。

B : Me, too.
我也是。

very

['vɛrɪ]
adv. 很、非常

例句

It's very warm today.
今天很暖和。

Our bus is moving very slowly.
我們的公車開得非常慢。

會話

A : Allow me.
我來處理！

B : Thanks a lot. It's very kind of you.
多謝啦！你真是好心。

A : It's beautiful, isn't it?
好漂亮，對吧？

B : Yes, it is.
沒錯，的確是的！

finally

['faɪnḷɪ]
adv. 最後地、最終地

同 義 eventually adv. 最後地、最終地

例句

He finally found his key in the second drawer.
最後他在第二個抽屜找到了他的鑰匙。

After several long delays, the plane finally left at 8 o'clock.
在幾次長時間耽誤以後，飛機最後在八點鐘起飛。

會話

A : What decision did you finally make?
你們最後做出了什麼決定？

B : We decided to give it up.
我們決定要放棄了。

A : What about David? What's his decision?
大衛呢？他的決定是什麼？

B : He finally changed his mind.
他終於改變他的想法了。

sometimes

['sʌm,taɪmz]
adv. 有時地、不時地

例句

Sometimes he comes by train and sometimes by car.
他有時搭火車來，有時坐汽車來。

Sometimes we go shopping.
有的時候我們去逛街購物。

會話

A : Do you think I'm crazy?
你覺得我瘋了嗎？

B : Sometimes.
有的時候你是的！

A : What do you usually do on Saturday?
你們星期六通常都在做什麼？

B : Sometimes we go to a movie.
有的時候我們去看電影。

what

[hwat]
adv. 在哪一方、到什麼程度
pron. 什麼、怎麼樣
adj. 什麼、多麼

例句

What am I supposed to do?
我應該怎麼做？

What a pity!
真遺憾！

會話

A : What color is your car?
你的車是什麼顏色？

B : It's black.
是黑色的。

A : What a wuss.
真是朝三暮四的人。

B : How can you say that?
你怎麼能這麼說？

when

[hwɛn]
adv. 什麼時候、何時
conj. 當…的時候
pron. 何時

例句

When will they come?
他們什麼時候會來？

It was eleven when I went to bed.
我是在十一點鐘上床的。

會話

A : When do you want to come?
你想什麼時候來？

B : How about this Friday?
這個星期五怎麼樣？

A : I got engaged to Maria when travelling last winter.
去年冬天旅行時，我和瑪麗亞訂婚了。

B : Congratulations.
恭喜你！

where

[hwɛr]
adv. 在哪裡、在…地方
pron. 何處

例句

Where are you going?
你要去哪裡？

Where to?
去哪裡？（計程車司機用語）

會話

A : What did you say to Jenny?
你對珍妮說了什麼？

B : I asked her where to put it.
我問她要放在哪裡。

A : Where did you see David?
你在哪裡看見大衛的？

B : I saw him at the MRT entrance.
我在捷運出口看見他。

why

[hwaɪ]

adv. 為什麼、理由、所以…的原因

例句

Why did you think so?
你為什麼會這麼認為？

They asked him why he was so dirty.
他們問他怎麼弄得這麼髒。

會話

A : May I come in?
我可以進來嗎？

B : Why not?
請進！

A : Why do you say so?
你為什麼要這麼說？

B : What else do you want me to say?
不然你要我說什麼？

again

[ə'gɛn]
adv. 再一次、再、又（恢復原狀）

例句

Please say it again.
請再說一遍。

She was ill. But now she's well again.
她曾生過病，但現在她已經康復。

會話

A : Come again?
你說什麼？

B : I said my name is David White.
我說我的名字是大衛・懷特。

A : Would you try again later?
你可以稍後再試一下嗎？

B : Sure. I will.
好的！我會的！

off

[ɔf]
adv. 離去、停了、（時間、空間的）距離
prep. 從…脫離

例句

They got into the car and drove off.
他們上了車就開走了。

She turned off the lights.
她關了燈。

會話

A : Where is the station?
車站在哪裡？

B : Get on this bus and get off at the station.
搭這輛公車，到車站下車。

A : How far is the town?
小鎮有多遠？

B : The town is five miles off.
小鎮離這裡有五英里遠。

out

[aʊt]

adv. 離開、向外、在外、大聲地、昏迷

反 義 in adv. **進、在裡面、在家**

例句

Let's go out for a walk.
我們出去散散步吧！

The bells rang out.
鐘聲響起。

會話

A : Where is Tom?
湯姆在哪裡？

B : He just went out.
他剛剛出去了。

A : Can I talk to David?
我可以和大衛講電話嗎？

B : Sorry, he's out of the office.
抱歉，他不在辦公室。

單字附錄

人稱 subject

我	I
我們	we
他	he
她	she
他們	they
你（們）	you
它	it

所有格 possessive case

我的	my
我們的	our

他的	his
她的	her
他們的	their
你（們）的	your
它的	its

親屬 family

祖父、外公	grandfather
祖母、外婆	grandmother
祖父母、外祖父母	grandparent
父母	parents
父親	father
母親	mother
公公、岳父	father-in-law
婆婆、岳母	mother-in-law

伯父、叔父、舅舅	uncle
伯母、嬸嬸、舅母	aunt
丈夫	husband
妻子	wife
兄弟	brother
姐妹	sister
手足	sibling
堂／表兄妹	cousin
女婿	son-in-law
媳婦	daughter-in-law
姊夫、妹夫、連襟、丈夫／妻子之兄弟	brother-in-law
嫂嫂、弟媳、妯娌、丈夫／妻子之姊妹	sister-in-law
小孩	kid=child
兒子	son

女兒	daughter
孫子	grandson
孫女	granddaughter
外甥、姪兒	nephew
甥女、姪女	niece

顏色 color

深色	dark
淺色	light
金色	gold
黑色	black
白色	white
灰色	gray
銀色	silver
紅色	red

橙色	orange
黃色	yellow
褐色	brown
綠色	green
藍色	blue
靛色	indigo
紫色	purple

星期 week

星期一	Monday(縮寫 Mon.)
星期二	Tuesday(縮寫 Tue.)
星期三	Wednesday(縮寫 Wed.)
星期四	Thursday(縮寫 Thu.)
星期五	Friday(縮寫 Fri.)
星期六	Saturday(縮寫 Sat.)

星期日	Sunday(縮寫 Sun.)

月份 month

一月	January (縮寫 Jan.)
二月	February(縮寫 Feb.)
三月	March(縮寫 Mar.)
四月	April(縮寫 Apr.)
五月	May
六月	June(縮寫 Jun.)
七月	July(縮寫 Jul.)
八月	August(縮寫 Aug.)
九月	September(縮寫 Sep.)
十月	October(縮寫 Oct.)
十一月	November(縮寫 Nov.)
十二月	December(縮寫 Dec.)

季節 season

春天	spring
夏天	summer
秋天	autumn=fall
冬天	winter
氣溫	temperature
攝氏	Celsius
華氏	Fahrenheit

房間 room

客廳	living room
衣櫃間	walk-in closet
餐廳	dining room
餐具室	pantry

起居室	parlor
臥室	bedroom
客房	guest room
廚房	kitchen
浴廁	bathroom
淋浴間	shower
車庫	garage
庭院	garden
閣樓	attic
地窖	cellar
書房	atelier
儲藏室	storeroom
地下室	basement
工作室	workshop
工具房	shed

設施 facilities

門廊	lobby
大門	front door
側門	side door
後門	back door
玄關	entrance hall
通道	aisle/entryway
走廊	porch/corridor
樓層	floor
樓梯	stairs
樓梯間	staircase
階梯	step
一樓	first floor
二樓	second floor
三樓	third floor

四樓	fourth floor
天花板	ceiling
陽台	balcony
欄杆	banisters
門鈴	doorbell
信箱	mailbox
屋頂	roof
車道	driveway
煙囪	chimney
壁爐	fireplace

電器 electric appliance

電視機	TV set
音響	stereo
擴音機	speaker

收音機	radio
空調	air-conditioning
電熱器	electric heater
暖氣機	heater
風扇	fan
空氣清淨機	air cleaner
增濕機	humidifier
除濕機	dehumidifier
冷氣機	air conditioner

廚房用具 kitchenware

爐子	stove
瓦斯爐	gas stove
微波爐	microwave
冰箱	refrigerator

冷凍庫	freezer
烤箱	oven
電鍋	electric rice cooker
熱水瓶	thermos
抽風機	exhaust fan
抽油煙機	range hood
通風機	ventilator

餐具 tableware

器皿	utensil
銀餐具	silverware
餐刀	knife
牛排刀	steak knife
叉子	fork
碗	bowl

筷子	chopsticks
盤子	dish
湯匙	spoon
湯杓	ladle
大湯匙	tablespoon
小調羹	teaspoon
瓶子	bottle
咖啡壺	coffeepot
咖啡杯	coffee cup
杯子	cup
水杯	glass
酒杯	wineglass
茶壺	teapot
壺、罐	pitcher

超市 supermarket

購物手推車	shopping cart
提籃	basket
磅秤	scale
區域	section
置物架	shelf
走道	aisle
冷凍食品	frozen foods
肉類	meat
海鮮類	seafood
蔬菜類	vegetable
水果	fruit
烘烤食品	bakery
穀類	cereal
乳製品	dairy

罐頭食品	canned goods

肉類 meat

牛肉	beef
牛排	steak
羊肉	mutton
小羊肉	lamb
豬肉	pork
雞肉	chicken
火雞肉	turkey
鴨肉	duck
鵝肉	goose
排骨	chop
羊排	lamb chop
豬排	pork chop

燉肉	stew
烤肉	roast
肉絲	shredded meat
絞肉	ground meat
肉片	cutlet
瘦肉	lean meat
肥肉	fatty meat
火腿	ham
香腸	sausage
培根	bacon

海鮮 seafood

魚	fish
烏魚	mullet
旗魚	sailfish

鯷魚	anchovy
鮭魚	salmon
鯊魚	shark
鯉魚	carp
鯰魚	catfish
鰱魚	chub
鰻魚	eel
鱈魚	cod
鱒魚	trout
鱸魚	perch
比目魚	flounder
沙丁魚	sardine
金魚	goldfish
金槍魚	tuna
青魚、鯡魚	herring
紅鯛魚	red snapper

海鱸魚	sea bass
烏賊	cuttlefish
章魚	octopus
魷魚、墨魚	squid
蛤蜊	clam
蚌類	mussel
扇貝	scallop
牡蠣	oyster
蝦	shrimp
明蝦	prawn
小龍蝦	crayfish
龍蝦	lobster
螃蟹	crab

蔬菜 vegetables

紅蘿蔔	carrot
蘿蔔	radish
洋蔥	onion
洋芋	potato(pl. potatoes)
甘薯	sweet potato
芋頭	taro
甜菜	beet
甜菜根	beetroot
包心菜	cabbage
花椰菜	cauliflower
甘藍菜	kale
芹菜	celery
萵苣	lettuce
菠菜	spinach
青椒	green pepper
黃瓜	cucumber

小黃瓜	gherkin
南瓜	pumpkin
苦瓜	bitter gourd
絲瓜	sponge gourd
香瓜	melon
玉米	corn
茄子	eggplant
豌豆	pea
菜豆	bean
青豆	green bean
豆芽菜	bean sprout
秋葵	okra
竹筍	bamboo
大蒜	garlic
青蔥	green onion
胡椒	pepper

香菜	cilantro
薄荷	mint
茴香	fennel
荷蘭芹	parsley(pl. parsleys)
韭菜	leek
黑橄欖	black olive
蕃茄	tomato(pl. tomatoes)
香菇	mushroom
蘆筍	asparagus

水果 fruit

木瓜	papaya
椰子	coconut
甘蔗	sugarcane
西瓜	watermelon

蘋果	apple
桃子	peach(pl. peaches)
梨子	pear
棗子	date
無花果	fig
番石榴	guava
李子	plum
芒果	mango(pl. mangoes)
香橙	orange
橘子	mandarin orange
奇異果	kiwi
柿子	persimmon
胡桃	walnut
香蕉	banana
桑椹	mulberry
栗子	chestnut

葡萄柚	grapefruit
鳳梨	pineapple
檸檬	lemon
萊姆	lime
葡萄	grape
草莓	strawberry(pl. strawberries)
蔓越莓	cranberry
藍莓	blueberry
覆盆莓	raspberry
櫻桃	cherry(pl. cherries)
杏仁	almond
穀物	cereal
燕麥	oat
麥子	wheat
燕麥粥	oatmeal
米穀物	rice cereal

大麥	barley
糙米	whole grain rice

速食 fast food

垃圾食物	junk food
菜單	menu
點餐	order
漢堡	hamburger
炸雞	fried chicken
雞塊	chicken nuggets
薯條	French fries
熱狗	hot dog
汽水	soft drink
爆米花	popcorn
可樂	Cola

可口可樂	Coke
百事可樂	Pepsi
咖啡	coffee
大杯（飲料）	large
小杯（飲料）	small
奶精	cream
糖	sugar
蕃茄醬	ketchup
芥末醬	mustard
吸管	straw
紙巾	paper napkins
拖盤	tray

飲料 drinks

冷飲	cold drinks

飲料	beverage
酒精飲料	alcohol
水	water
礦泉水	mineral water
氣泡式礦泉水	sparkling water
茶	tea
濃茶	strong tea
淡茶	weak tea
紅茶	black tea
冰紅茶	iced black tea
巧克力奶昔	chocolate shake
果汁	juice
蘋果汁	apple juice
柳橙汁	orange juice
檸檬汁	lemonade
咖啡	coffee

葡萄酒	wine
牛奶	milk

口味 flavor

營養	nutrition
胃口	appetite
口渴的	thirsty
飢餓的	starving
飢餓的	hungry
飽食的	full
貪嘴的	greedy
美味的	delicious
色香味俱佳	savory
難吃的	yucky
好吃的	yummy

酸的	sour
（水果的）酸	tart
醋酸	vinegary
甜的	sweet
苦的	bitter
辛辣的、加香料的	spicy
辣的	hot
鹹的	salty
清淡的	light
（食物等）清淡的	plain
水分充足	watery
脆的	crispy
油膩的	rich/oily
難消化的	heavy
腐壞的	rotten
臭味的	stinking

燒焦的	burnt
沒味道	tasteless
未煮熟的	raw
（肉等）咬不動的	tough
（肉等）嫩的	tender

甜點 dessert

餅乾	cookie
麵包	bread
長麵包	loaf
土司	toast
蛋糕	cake
起司蛋糕	cheese cake
海綿蛋糕	sponge cake
戚風蛋糕	chiffon cake

糖果	candy (pl. candies)
三明治	sandwich
潛水艇堡	submarine sandwich
熱狗	hot dog
香蕉船	banana split
甜甜圈	doughnut
披薩	pizza
派	pie
蛋塔	egg tart
洋蔥圈	onion ring
炸花枝圈	fried calamari
烤肉串	shish kebab
薄脆餅乾	cracker
爆米花	popcorn
洋芋片	potato chips
玉米片	tortilla chips

優格	yogurt
冰淇淋	ice cream
聖代	sundae
零食	snack
巧克力	chocolate
布丁	pudding
蜜餞	compote

服裝 clothes

服裝	costume
正式服裝	dress
燕尾服	tailcoat
長袍	tunic
大衣	coat
外套	jacket

風衣	outer coat
雨衣	raincoat
休閒服	casual clothes
短袖圓領衫	T-shirt
牛仔裝	jeans
牛仔褲	jeans-pants
馬球衫	polo shirt
無袖背心	tank
背心	vest
男裝	suit
西裝	business suit
襯衫	shirt
褲子	pants
寬鬆的長褲	slacks
領帶	tie
女用襯衫	blouse

洋裝	dress
毛衣	sweater
裙子	skirt
迷你裙	miniskirt
制服	uniform
尿布	diaper
童裝	children's wear
浴衣	bathrobe
泳衣	swimwear
游泳衣褲	swim suit
游泳褲	bathing trunks
比基尼泳衣	bikini
睡衣	pajamas
【美俗】胸罩	bra
內衣	underwear
汗衫	undershirt

四角褲	boxer
三角褲（男女適穿）	brief
女短內褲	panties
飾品	accessory
珠寶	jewelry
珍珠	pearl
鑽石	diamond
黃金	gold
玉、翡翠	jade
胸針	brooch
胸花	corsage
袖扣	cuff link
別針	pin
耳環	earring
項鍊	necklace
手鐲	bracelet

戒指	ring

個人物品 personal item

帽子	hat
手套	gloves
頭巾	knitted shawl
頭巾	hood
領巾	scarf
披肩、圍巾	wrap
毛圍巾	wool scarf
大披巾	shawl
手帕	handkerchief
頭巾	turban
眼鏡	glasses
太陽眼鏡	sun glasses

手錶	watch(pl. watches)
雨傘	umbrella
袋子	bag
背包	backpack
錢包	purse
皮夾	wallet
手提箱	suitcase

襪子 & 鞋子 hosiery & shoes

短襪	socks
長襪	stockings
高跟鞋	high heels
皮鞋	leather shoes
休閒鞋	casual shoes
運動鞋	sports shoes

跑步鞋	running shoes
網球鞋	tennis shoes
靴子	boots
拖鞋	slippers
涼鞋	sandals

數量 quantity

一袋豆子	a bag of beans
一束花	a bouquet of flowers
一束玫瑰	a bouquet of roses
一箱蘋果	a box of apples
一串葡萄	a bunch of grapes
一串鑰匙	a bunch of keys
一塊條型巧克力	a bar of chocolate
一罐起司	a can of cheese

一瓶蕃茄醬	a bottle of ketchup
一盒菸	a carton of cigarettes
一桶啤酒	a tub of beer
一球冰淇淋	a tub of ice cream
一打蛋	a dozen of eggs
一條麵包	a loaf of bread
一盒柳橙汁	a carton of orange juice
一段口香糖	a stick of chewing gum
一串香蕉	a hand of bananas
一杯水	a glass of water
一點鹽	a touch of salt
一捲壁紙	a piece of wallpaper
一張紙	a piece of paper
一把剪刀	a pair of scissors
一個圓規	a pair of compasses
一盎司的牛奶	an ounce of milk

一公升的酒	a liter of wine
一夸脫的油	a quart of oil
一加侖的牛奶	a gallon of milk
一磅的砂糖	a pound of sugar
一瓣大蒜	a clove of garlic
一團毛線	a ball of wool

公共地區 public place

首都	capital
大都市	metropolis
市中心	downtown
法院	court
銀行	bank
郵局	post office
學校	school

圖書館	library
車站	station
機場	airport
港口	port
教堂	church
大教堂	cathedral
小禮拜堂	chapel
墓地	cemetery
動物園	zoo
公園	park
草地	lawn
劇院	theater
電影院	cinema
俱樂部	club
博物館	museum
美術館	art museum

畫廊	art gallery
醫院	hospital
體育場	stadium
健身房	gym
游泳池	swimming pool
紀念碑	monument
公車站	bus station
地鐵	subway
捷運站	metro station
計程車招呼站	taxi stand
停車場	parking lot
加油站	gas station

娛樂 entertainments

玩耍	play

唱歌	sing
跳舞	dance
繪畫	paint
運動	exercise
游泳	swimming
棋	chess
牌	playing cards
球	ball
遊戲	game
遊樂場	amusement center
馬戲團	fairground
摩天輪	Ferris wheel
旋轉木馬	merry-go-round
溜滑梯	slide
蹺蹺板	seesaw
盪鞦韆	swing

交通工具 conveyance

自行車	bike/bicycle
機車	motorcycle
【美口語】三輪車	wheel
四輪馬車	carriage
車輛	vehicle
汽車	car
轎車	sedan
客貨兩用車	wagon
小貨車	van
休旅車	recreational vehicle (縮寫 RV)
計程車	taxicab/cab
吉普車	jeep
卡車	truck
公車	bus (pl. buses)

地下鐵	subway
電車	trolley
火車	train
捷運	metro
纜車	tram
小船	boat
船	ship
遊艇、帆船	yacht
大船	vessel
飛機	plane
直升飛機	helicopter
熱氣球	hot-air balloon

交通 traffic

駕駛	drive

駕駛員	driver
乘客	passenger
減速	slow down
煞車	break
迴轉	turn around
倒車	reverse
靠邊停車	pullover
左轉	turn left
右轉	turn right
通過、經過	pass
橫越	cross
橫過地	across
交通堵塞	traffic jam
車禍	car accident
小車禍	fender bender
汽車撞成一堆	pileup

（汽車的）猛撞	crash(pl. crashes)
衝撞、顛簸行進	bump
碰撞	collision
傷害	injury
中斷	interruption
擁擠	congestion
繞道	detour
罰單	ticket
違規停車罰單	parking ticket
超速罰單	speeding ticket
目的地	destination

距離 distance

哩	mile
公里	kilometer

遠／遠的	far
近／近的	close
靠近的	near
長／長的	long
短／短的	short
更遠的	farther
最遠的	farthest
更近的	closer
最近的	closest
更近的	nearer
最近的	nearest
更長的	longer
最長的	longest
更短的	shorter
最短的	shortest
走路	walk

捷徑	shortcut
方向	direction
東	east
西	west
南	south
北	north

學校 school

大學	university
學院	college
學院	institute
高中	senior high school
國中	junior high school
小學	primary school
幼童學校	infant school

幼稚園	kindergarten
托兒所	day nursery
圖書室	library
保健室	health center
老師	teacher
學生	student
同學	classmate
班級	class
學習	study
考試	test
小考	quiz
詢問	ask
問題	question
回答	answer
畢業	graduate

頭部 head

臉部	face
頭髮	hair
額頭	forehead
太陽穴	temple
眉毛	eyebrow
眼睛	eye
眼窩	eyehole
眼瞼、眼皮	eyelid
睫毛	eyelashes
瞳孔	pupil
耳朵	ear
耳垂	earlobe
鼻子	nose
鼻孔	nostril

臉頰	cheek
嘴	mouth
嘴唇	lip
顎	jaw
上顎	upper jaw
下顎	lower jaw
下巴	chin
牙齒	tooth (pl. teeth)
舌頭	tongue
鬍子	mustache
絡腮鬍	whisker
鬢角	sideburns

手臂 arm

腋下	armpit

肘部	elbow
手	hand
手掌	palm
手背	back
手腕	wrist
拳頭	fist
手指	finger
大拇指	thumb
食指	forefinger/first finger
中指	middle finger
無名指	third finger
小指	little finger
手指甲	fingernail
指甲	nail

腿 leg

大腿	lap
膝蓋	knee
小腿	shank
小腿肚	calf
踝	ankle
腳	foot(pl. feet)
腳趾頭	toe
腳趾甲	toenail
腳背	instep
腳後跟	heel
腳底	sole
腳掌心	arch

身體 body

頭	head
腦	brain
咽喉	throat
扁桃腺	tonsil
脖子	neck
後頸	nape
胸部、乳房	chest
乳頭	nipple
腹部	abdomen
肚臍	navel
肩	shoulder
背	back
腰	waist
臀部	hip

屁股的半邊肉	buttocks
屁股（俗語）	butt
皮膚	skin
肌肉	muscle
骨頭	bones
頭蓋骨	skull
鎖骨	collarbone
肋骨	rib
脊骨、脊柱	backbone
胸骨	breastbone
關節	joint
指關節	knuckle
膝蓋骨	kneecap
骨盆	pelvis
腱	sinew
骨骼	skeleton

血管	veins
靜脈	vein
動脈	artery
神經	nerve
脊髓	spinal marrow

器官 organ

心臟	heart
腎臟	kidney
肺	lung
肝	liver
膽囊	gallbladder
隔膜	diaphragm
食道	gullet
胃	stomach

胰腺	pancreas
脾	spleen
十二指腸	duodenum
大腸	large intestine
小腸	small intestine
直腸	rectum
盲腸	appendix
膀胱	bladder
肛門	anus
尿道	urine
陰莖	penis
睪丸	testicle
卵巢	ovary
子宮	womb
陰道	vagina
疾病	disease

病症	symptoms
疾病	illness
生病的	sick
頭痛	headache
瞎的	blind
耳聾的	deaf
打嗝	burp
吐	vomit
咳嗽	cough
鼻塞、胸悶	congested
牙痛	toothache
蛀牙	cavity
打噴嚏	sneeze
臉色蒼白	pale
營養不良	malnutrition
感冒	cold

流感	flu
胃痛	stomachache
腹瀉	diarrhea
瘧疾	malaria
麻疹	measles
癌症	cancer

受傷 hurt

使受傷 / 受傷	hurt
傷殘	injuries
流血	bleed
腫脹的	swollen
扭傷、挫傷	twist
使扭傷	sprain
使脫臼	dislocate

使瘀傷／瘀青	bruise
切、剪／傷口	cut
傷口、創傷	wound
折斷	break
抓、搔	scratch
擦、刮	scrape
癢	itch
發癢的	itchy

無敵英語1500句生活會話 (48開)

史上超強、實用英文會話文庫！！
用最簡單的英文會話，就可以流利的表達。
本書彙整超過1500句的生活常用會話語句，
讓您的英文口語能力突飛猛進！

無敵英語1500單字 (48開)

史上超強、實用英文單字字庫！！
單字不是會背就好，還必須應用在會話中。
本書將單字套用在會話中，
只要花一半的時間，
同時記住單字和英語會話。

How do you do 最實用的生活英語 (25開)

當問候朋友時　How do you do?
當發生危急事件時　Somebody, help!
當不認同對方所言時　I don’t think so.
當讚美對方的表現時　Good job.
當想要離職時　I quit.
你還想要說的英語有哪些？本書通通有！

國家圖書館出版品預行編目資料

1000基礎實用單字 / 張瑜凌編著. -- 初版.
-- 新北市 : 雅典文化, 民101.10
面 ; 公分. -- (全民學英文 ; 28)
ISBN 978-986-6282-67-6(平裝附光碟片)
1.英語 2.詞彙 3.會話

805.12 101015795

全民學英文系列 28

1000基礎實用單字

編著/張瑜凌
責編/張瑜凌
美術編輯/蕭若辰
封面設計/劉逸芹

法律顧問：方圓法律事務所/涂成樞律師

總經銷：永續圖書有限公司
永續圖書線上購物網
www.foreverbooks.com.tw

CVS代理/美璟文化有限公司
TEL：(02) 2723-9968
FAX：(02) 2723-9668

出版日/2012年10月

雅典文化

出版社
22103 新北市汐止區大同路三段194號9樓之1
TEL (02) 8647-3663
FAX (02) 8647-3660

全民
學英文
28

1000基礎實用單字

雅致風靡　典藏文化

親愛的顧客您好，感謝您購買這本書。即日起，填寫讀者回函卡寄回至本公司，我們每月將抽出一百名回函讀者，寄出精美禮物並享有生日當月購書優惠！想知道更多更即時的消息，歡迎加入"永續圖書粉絲團"

您也可以選擇傳真、掃描或用本公司準備的免郵回函寄回，謝謝。

傳真電話：（02）8647-3660　　電子信箱：yungjiuh@ms45.hinet.net

姓名：　　性別：□男　□女

出生日期：　年　月　日　電話：

學歷：　　職業：□男　□女

E-mail：

地址：□□□

從何處購買此書：　　購買金額：　　元

購買本書動機：□封面 □書名 □排版 □內容 □作者 □偶然衝動

你對本書的意見：

內容：□滿意□尚可□待改進　編輯：□滿意□尚可□待改進

封面：□滿意□尚可□待改進　定價：□滿意□尚可□待改進

其他建議：

剪下後傳真、掃描或寄回至「22103新北市汐止區大同路3段194號9樓之1雅典文化收」

您可以使用以下方式將回函寄回。

您的回覆，是我們進步的最大動力，謝謝。

① 使用本公司準備的免郵回函寄回。

② 傳真電話：（02）8647-3660

③ 掃描圖檔寄到電子信箱：

yungjiuh@ms45.hinet.net

沿此線對折後寄回，謝謝。

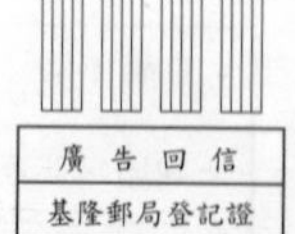

廣告回信
基隆郵局登記證
基隆廣字第056號

2 2 1-0 3

雅典文化事業有限公司　收

新北市汐止區大同路三段194號9樓之1

雅致風靡　典藏文化